The test

"Jamie is going to jump the big oak tree at Black Angel Bridge, and you know what that means. Right?" Kai said firmly.

"I think it's great!" Zoe said. "But she's never been there. She won't know how to do it, and it's really dangerous."

"What could be so dangerous?" Jamie asked with false bravado.

"The river is only deep in the middle," Zoe warned. "If you let go too soon or too late, you could break both your legs by jumping into the shallow water."

Kai shrugged, looking at Jamie. "My sisters and some of their friends did it. We've done it. It's part of the deal. Are you still up for it?"

"Of course I'm up for it," Jamie said with a reckless smile. "I'm not afraid of any old bridge or tree." She clenched her fists so that her fingernails were hidden in her palms and felt her stomach turn over like an egg in a skillet.

Other Knopf Paperbacks you will enjoy:

Ellie & the Bunheads
by Sally Warner

The Junkyard Dog
by Erika Tamar

Sammy Keyes and the Hotel Thief
by Wendelin Van Draanen

Songs of Faith
by Angela Johnson

Starting School with an Enemy
by Elisa Carbone

Dona Schenker

THE SECRET CIRCLE

A KNOPF PAPERBACK

ALFRED A. KNOPF ▸ NEW YORK

A KNOPF PAPERBACK PUBLISHED BY ALFRED A. KNOPF

www.randomhouse.com/kids

Library of Congress Cataloging-in-Publication Data
Schenker, Dona
The Secret Circle / by Dona Schenker.
p.   cm.
Summary: Sixth grader Jamie enters a new school and must decide if membership to
an exclusive clique, The Secret Circle, is worth the price of betraying a friend.
[1. Friendship — Fiction. 2. Schools — Fiction.] I. Title.
PZ7.S34356Sg   1998
[Fic] — dc21   98-10035

ISBN 0-679-88989-2 (trade)
ISBN 0-679-98989-7 (lib. bdg.)
ISBN 0-375-80354-8 (pbk.)

First Knopf Paperback edition: July 2000
Printed in the United States of America
10 9 8 7 6 5 4 3 2

The Secret Circle is dedicated to my beloved mother,
Rosemary Alexander, in gratitude for all she taught me.

Acknowledgments

To Andrea Cascardi, my talented editor. Thank you.

To my sons, Alex and Max, and my husband, Cecil.
You are always completely supportive, and I love you.

To many friends, old and new, who daily enrich my life.

To the Glass clan and my aunt Peggy.
I'm so proud you are my family.

To my writing friends, Paul Zindel, Kim Little, and Diane Burns.

To John Worsham, my confidant, collaborator, and trusted friend.
You are a treasure.

And to Dr. Steiner, wherever you are.

Chapter ONE

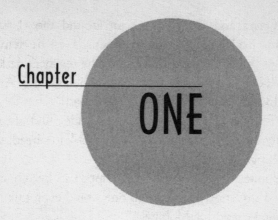

I have no friends, Jamie McClure thought, and now Pearlie Wu is dead.

Behind her Theresa O'Malley whispered across the aisle to Abigail Frank. "Something is going to happen today. Can't you just feel it?"

Jamie swiveled around to hear.

"Something happens every day," Abigail answered. "Why would this one be any different?" Both girls ignored Jamie as usual and went on whispering.

Jamie looked for signs of excitement around the sixth-grade classroom of her new school, St. Agnes Hall for Girls. The late bell rang, sending most of the girls to their desks. An ancient white cat with a pushed-in face strolled through the doorway as it had done every day since school started two weeks ago. Only today the fur between his ears and neck was completely gone except for a thin strip down the middle that stood straight up.

"Look at Lump!" Frederika Potts shouted. "Who gave Lump a Mohawk?"

Gasps and giggles went up around the classroom. Lump made an outrageous spectacle as he lumbered across the room and jumped onto the teacher's desk.

"Poor Lump," Jamie said to Theresa and Abigail. "Why would anyone shave Lump's head?"

Theresa stared at Lump in wonder and shrugged. Abigail turned her palms up and shook her head, saying nothing.

Jamie turned around and slumped in her chair. She hated this snotty school. No one would even talk to her about a cat with a Mohawk.

Mr. Vincent Hughes-Walter came in, papers hanging out of his briefcase. When he saw Lump, now dozing on top of his desk, he gingerly lifted the cat's head to get a better look. He turned incredulously to the class.

"Is this someone's idea of a joke?" he demanded. "Who did this?"

He looked up and down the rows and stared at the back of the room where the St. Claire twins, Vivica and Merit, were still huddled with Kai Standish and Zoe Warner. They were usually together and formed a captivating pack, at least to Jamie. Even their names, which she'd memorized at roll call, were unique. Vivica had a rounded chin, while Merit's was pointed, making them easy to tell apart.

"It could be anyone," Vivica said, taking her seat. "Lump doesn't belong to the school. He just hangs around St. Agnes because the ladies in the kitchen feed him."

"And you give him kitty treats, Mr. Hughes-Walter," her twin teased. "That's why he's always in our room."

"I merely reward him for good behavior," Mr. Hughes-Walter said.

"Lump's too old and tired to be bad," Theresa said. "I feel sorry for him. He'll walk around like that for weeks until his fur grows out."

"It's not like he really cares what he looks like," said Kai.

"Still," Theresa murmured.

Just then, from a box above the clock, Headmistress Pickney told the girls to stand. She led the school in the Pledge of Allegiance and talked about the soccer schedule.

Jamie's mind wandered and she scanned the room. It wasn't the first time she was struck by the difference between the way the girls in class looked and the way they behaved. Each white shirt in the class appeared painstakingly ironed, the creases knife-sharp across the shoulders and down the sleeves. Every green and white plaid skirt was pleated, and dark green socks stopped just below each girl's knees. Even Mr. Hughes-Walter wore a dark green blazer with a St. Agnes crest on the pocket.

When the class was seated, Mr. Hughes-Walter, still shaking his head, called roll.

"Let's get right down to work," he grimly said, and strode to a cabinet at the side of the room. He twirled a combination lock back and forth until it opened. He'd had the cabinet installed the second day of school and put a combination lock on it.

Mr. Vincent Hughes-Walter was secretive by nature, Jamie decided. She had seen him on the street late one afternoon after school. A tall, thin man, he hurried along, his head down. Her mother stopped him and reintroduced herself. He colored at each of her mother's polite questions. The only information they learned was that he was just out of college, did not like the Texas heat, and lived with his aunt.

It was only when Mr. Hughes-Walter talked about something he was interested in that he seemed at ease. Unfortunately for Jamie, he was most interested in science and math. His idea of classroom pets were white mice with beady pink eyes and his large box turtle, Billy. Mrs. Lamprey, the teacher across the hall, had a fluffy guinea pig and a baby ferret.

Mr. Hughes-Walter took papers from the cabinet, snapped the lock closed, and twirled the numbers on the face. "By the time I've finished teaching this lesson, microscopic portions of my mouth will be all over your clothes. In fact, they will be *everywhere in this room*," he suddenly announced with a smile.

"Eeeuw!" and "Ughh!" the girls said loudly, making throwing-up noises.

Mr. Hughes-Walter appeared surprised by the outburst. He pulled his chin to the back of his neck and let out a long, whistling sigh between his teeth.

"Let's act our age and not our shoe size," he said.

He quickly passed papers down the rows of the classroom. The papers showed a diagram of the human mouth and throat. "Human saliva carries more germs than any other animal's," Mr. Hughes-Walter said. "Who can tell me why?"

Frederika Potts raised her hand, "Because humans put their fingers in their mouths?" she asked.

Mr. Hughes-Walter went into a long explanation of

why this was only partially true. He moved about the front of the room, drawing on the board, his long legs always in motion, bending like straps.

"Now," he finally announced, "complete your assignment by putting the words on the board into their proper spaces on your diagram."

Spit, Jamie thought, and sighed. I am learning about spit first thing in the morning. Mother scrimped and saved and took on even more catering jobs so that I can go to this expensive school with the daughters of the people she cooks for. I have no friends, and odd things happen all the time, and now Pearlie Wu is dead.

She felt the same choking disbelief that filled her every time she thought of her favorite neighbor's sudden death over the weekend of blood poisoning from a cut along her arm. A chill, a fever, sudden sweats—little things. They called it septicemia after she died. Pearlie never even thought to go to a doctor.

The morning sun flickered across the walls of the classroom. Jamie copied the words "sublingual gland" and "submandibular gland" from the blackboard onto the proper space on her diagram. She was about to write down "parotid gland" when Kai Standish went to Mr. Hughes-Walter's desk.

Jamie had noticed Kai on the first day of school because her hair was cut like Jamie's little brother Gus's, very short, and it was fawn colored. She had tawny gold eyes, wild as a cat's. Carefree bangs fringed her forehead. This boy haircut reminded Jamie of the face of a youth in a medieval tapestry that hung in the library at the university.

"This is sort of embarrassing," Kai said to the teacher in a confidential but carrying tone. Her face flushed. "But, well...I'm afraid my watch is missing." Her voice was deep and hoarse for a twelve-year-old's.

Mr. Hughes-Walter's face contorted with surprise.

"Are you certain?" he asked.

"Positive," Kai answered. "I put it on my pencil box when I got to school. Then I went to wash my hands in the bathroom. I just realized it's gone. I hate to think that someone took it, but..."

The air was suddenly charged with tension, and the room came alive with the buzz of a dozen conversations.

"Well, I'm sure it will turn up with your things today." Mr. Hughes-Walter cinched his tie up hard under his prominent Adam's apple.

"I'm sorry," Kai said, pouncing on his reluctance to pursue the issue. "I've looked everywhere. My grandmother gave it to me. I don't know what will happen if I come home without it." Her lower lip trembled convincingly.

Secretly Jamie wanted to laugh at the expression on Mr. Hughes-Walter's face. He sat erect in his chair, gripping the armrests; he looked like a man about to take off in a hurricane. When he finally rose, he spoke with exaggerated emphasis, as if they were first graders.

"Kai says that her watch is missing. She put it on her desk before school started and left it there when she went to the bathroom. Would you take a moment to look through your books and papers, class, and see if Kai's watch was mixed in by accident?" Mr. Hughes-Walter asked.

as if she were
too pretty to be her signature—
Mr. Hughes-Walter reached the adornment of hair.
and was immersed in the conve
messy desk. Kai

Walter said.

"No one should ⌐
said. "It's still here. I know ⌐

"Would it make you feel betu⌐
desks?" Mr. Hughes-Walter asked. He had ⌐

"Yes." Kai nodded her head.

Mr. Hughes-Walter sniffed and reluctantly said, "Please raise the lids of your desks, and I'll just have a quick peek."

Each student opened her desk while Mr. Hughes-Walter went down the rows. He bent his knees, lowered his prematurely balding head, and went through the belongings inside everyone's desk.

Kai was calm now, standing at the front of the room. She pushed her bangs with the tips of her fingers and absently stroked Lump's ears. She was completely relaxed, as if she knew, just by instinct, how to be. At once Jamie felt lanky and awkward.

Some of the girls in the class enlivened their uniforms with pins or scarves or wore ribbons around their ponytails. The twins wore lip gloss with a pink tint. Zoe had all that copper hair that even now flared rebelliously out of the braid she'd forced it into. But Kai was as plain

7

...nts of Frederika Potts's ... took something from her shirt pocket and slipped over to the combination lock on the cabinet.

Her back was to the class, so Jamie couldn't see what Kai was doing. Kai worked quickly, then walked calmly back to her desk, sat down, and opened her desktop.

Zoe fidgeted with the wire binding on her notebook. There was a funny look on her face. It was an expression people wore when they *knew* something.

The only sound came from the humming fluorescent lights and Mr. Hughes-Walter's rummaging until one of the twins covered what sounded like a burst of hysterical laughter by forcing a coughing fit.

"I found it!" Kai suddenly said. "It was in my pencil box." She dangled the watch triumphantly for the class to see. "I must have put it there and forgotten all about it. I'm so sorry, everybody. I really am, Mr. Hughes-Walter."

Mr. Hughes-Walter straightened his thin shoulders and looked relieved.

"All's well that ends well," he said. "We've wasted too much valuable class time, though. We'll have to move on to our English test."

"Oh, no," said Vivica. "You were going to tell us about those universe theories this morning."

"I was?" Mr. Hughes-Walter looked confused. He stared at the ceiling. "Oh, very well!" he said enthusiastically. He seems to have the attention span of a rabbit, Jamie thought.

"There are two main theories: steady state and big bang. Steady state says that the universe has always existed in its present form, but astronomical observations do not support the steady state theory." He bobbed across the front of the room, waving his arms. He drew an explosion on the board.

"Big bang says that the universe was created about eighteen billion years ago." His voice raced on and on about primordial fireballs and expansions.

Jamie's mind churned. She had the familiar feeling she'd had since coming to St. Agnes.

Strange things happened that everyone else seemed to think were hilarious or took for granted. On the first day of school white mice ran around in the space behind the radiator until the janitor finally lured them out with sunflower seeds. They dozed in their cages now, but how did they keep getting out? The next day they disturbed the class for an entire morning by scratching at the entrance to the heating vents. Mr. Hughes-Walter lost his lunch hour and ruined his slacks crawling around until he caught them.

The third day of school Frederika Potts screamed. Earthworms from the science class were digging through her desk. Merit fainted, or at least pretended to. Her twin, Vivica, giggled all that day.

Mr. Hughes-Walter brushed the chalk from his hands and strode to his cabinet. "We really must take this English test before gym class."

He reached for the padlock, held it in his hands for

several moments, then backed away as if it were a scorpion. Mr. Hughes-Walter's face went slack with shock. His eyes darted around the room.

"Someone has painted the numbers of my padlock black," he finally said, his voice so high and tight it seemed to curl at the edge.

A collective bewilderment rumbled through the classroom, which Jamie found amazing. Hadn't everyone seen Kai? This incident was directed straight at Mr. Hughes-Walter. Any minute now someone was bound to snitch, probably Frederika Potts. Frederika (whom Jamie already knew as one of Pearlie's friends) was the blabber-mouth type.

"Wipe it off," Theresa suggested.

Mr. Hughes-Walter rubbed the face of the padlock. "It's dry. It appears to be painted with black enamel."

He had a youthful singsong voice that made Jamie realize he was just the teacher's pet all grown up. He couldn't fathom these pranks.

He fiddled with the lock and threw up his hands. "I can't see the numbers, so I can't open the lock. My private effects, including the test, are inside that cabinet."

"That's terrible," said Kai earnestly.

All eyes turned toward Kai like a patch of marigolds turned toward the sun. She sat with her back arched and held her neck taut like a ballerina.

"Who did this?" Mr. Hughes-Walter asked with accusing, reproaching eyes. "I really want to know who did this." His face was full of humiliation and anger.

Faint sounds echoed in the corridors—the slap of oxfords, a door heaving closed, the far-off piping of the coach's whistle.

Mr. Hughes-Walter sighed in a fed-up way. "Well, someone must have seen who did this. I'm passing twenty pieces of scrap paper around. Surely someone will put the name of the culprit down."

A tiny shiver went through Jamie. She wrote a question mark on the paper, folded it, and sent it forward. I wouldn't want to be Kai, she thought. Someone will turn her in and she'll never know who, but it won't be me. I'm no tattletale.

Mr. Hughes-Walter gathered the folded papers and opened them one after the other. When he came to the last one, he took a couple of deep breaths. "I have no names here. None. Only a slip that has a circle drawn on it with 'Shh' written beside it. What is that supposed to mean?"

When there was no answer, he shook his head and continued to survey them with wide-eyed suspicion. "If the culprit doesn't come forward, we'll just wait here together after school until she does."

"But I have soccer practice," Vivica said.

"Me too," a sprinkling of others protested around the room.

"Besides," Abigail said, "it's Friday!"

"Pearlie Wu's funeral is this afternoon," Frederika Potts said. "I'm playing the piano."

She is? Jamie was surprised. Who would have asked her to play at the funeral?

"Pearlie Who?" asked Mr. Hughes-Walter.

"No," said Zoe Warner gently. "Not Pearlie Who, Pearlie *Wu.*"

Mr. Hughes-Walter was clearly confused. "Have I missed something? Has a student or a teacher died?"

"No," Zoe said. "Pearlie Wu was this nice Chinese lady who sold honey at a stand in Booger Hollow. A lot of people in San Lucas bought honey from her."

"I visited Pearlie all the time," Frederika said. "I know more than you do, Zoe. Just because the funeral is at your house..."

Abigail Frank gasped and blurted, "Well, Zoe can't help it if the funeral is at her house, Frederika. *All* the funerals are at her house."

After a gawky hesitation and an alarmed stare, Mr. Hughes-Walter said, "Why would you have funerals at your house, Zoe?"

"My family owns Warner's Funeral Home," Zoe said calmly. "We always have, and we live there, too."

"Why are you playing the piano at the funeral, Frederika?" Kai asked. "No offense, but you're only twelve."

Frederika had a flat moon face that colored easily. "I called Mr. He-he Graves and asked if I could play 'Amazing Grace.' He said, 'That's fine. I don't care.' Then my mother called Mr. Warner at the funeral home and asked him to arrange it. Besides, I'm sure Pearlie would have wanted me to."

"Mr. He-he?" A monkeylike frown flickered on Mr. Hughes-Walter's face. "Is that a Chinese name?"

Jamie took a deep breath. She'd never spoken up in class, but she felt a need to say *something*. "Mr. Graves isn't Chinese. Pearlie called him Mr. He-he because he doesn't smile or laugh much."

"Or the bee master," Frederika said. "Sometimes she called him the bee master."

The girls' disapproval of Frederika was so strong Jamie

12

thought she could smell it, a metallic odor. Frederika was right about one thing, though. Pearlie liked kids so much she'd want one to play at her funeral; even an obnoxious know-it-all like Frederika who wandered over to Booger Hollow every chance she got to buy honey and talk Pearlie's ear off.

Mr. Hughes-Walter shook his head. His eyes were still dark from his recent anger. "Okay. All right. I'm forced to overlook the padlock incident this time due to this sad funeral. But nothing of this nature must happen again. There will be serious consequences."

Jamie felt a ridiculous urge to apologize. She brushed it aside. After all, she hadn't done anything, and she couldn't tell on a fellow student. No one else had. Still, she felt sorry for Mr. Hughes-Walter. Even his name was backward.

Chapter

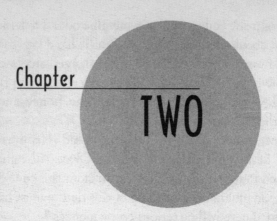

TWO

The air was heavy with the perfume of flowers in the packed funeral parlor. Sweat trickled down Jamie's back.

Frederika Potts sat at the piano, which was situated so that she faced the crowd. Her face was a big white dumpling of pride.

Jamie sat between her little brother, Gus, and her mother in the third row at the end of the aisle by the wall. She and Gus had never been to a funeral or even seen a dead person. Only a few days ago they had helped Pearlie Wu pour thick honey into jars and sell them at her roadside stand. Now, even at a distance of several yards and between the backs of the onlookers, Jamie could see inside the casket.

"I can see her nose in that coffin," Gus whispered. His eyes were enormous.

"And her chin, too," Jamie whispered back.

"I don't like this," Gus whimpered, forgetting to whisper.

"Shh," Jamie said.

The casket was gray, and it was submerged in lilies,

sprays of gladiolus, and red carnations. Jamie was filled with confusion and fear. She didn't want to look at the casket and feel the jump-jump of her heart, but she couldn't keep her eyes away.

The room was close and Jamie felt as though her insides were a nest of little snakes. What if I giggle? was her wild thought. If I can think it, I can do it, and Mother will kill me.

Gus stuck his finger into one of the diamond-shaped holes in the heating vent in the parlor floor. When he tried to get it out and couldn't, he looked up at Jamie with an oops expression. She reached down and yanked it out.

"Ow, Jamie," he whispered, and sucked his finger dramatically.

Mrs. McClure looked at them with a cold eye. "I know everyone in this room," she whispered in Jamie's ear. "Do *not* embarrass me."

Jamie felt a stab of anger. Why don't *you* ever sit by Gus, Mother? she wanted to say.

Gus settled back against his seat in the hushed chapel that was really the converted living room of the old Warner mansion on University Avenue. He tore off the corner of a page in his hymnal and placed it on the edge of his tongue. Jamie shook her head at him and tried to frown, but the impulse to laugh out loud was overwhelming.

Someone had brought a fat baby to the chapel. The room was so full of flowers that the baby sneezed again and again. In a loud voice the baby suddenly said, "Dahdeed!" Just then, a car rounded the street corner, making a shrieking sound.

"Is that the hearse?" Gus asked.

Gus had just started first grade. He clearly wanted to know. An image of a fast car that took dead people away at lightning speed rose up, and Jamie wondered where a crazy thought like that came from.

"No, Gus," she whispered.

At the front of the room on a stage above the casket was a podium where she supposed the minister would speak. On the other side of the podium Mr. Graves, Pearlie Wu's husband, and Miss Graves, his sister, sat in stiff armchairs. Mr. Graves wore a suit with a yellow rose in the lapel. It was true that Pearlie sometimes called him the bee master because he took care of the beehives on the property behind their house.

"I just hate open caskets," Mrs. McClure murmured to no one in particular.

"The casket. It's so small, like a child's," Jamie whispered back.

"Well, after all, she was shorter than you." At this, her mother looked at Jamie.

Who's *not* shorter than me? Jamie wanted to ask. This usually depressing thought struck her as screamingly funny, and she bit her tongue between her front teeth.

The minister rose and stepped slowly to the microphone. For a few moments there was complete silence. Jamie could hear the breathing of people, particularly those who breathed as heavily as old Mr. Jenner.

"One of God's quiet people, one of his lambs, has been called back," the minister began.

Gus elbowed Jamie and whispered, "Pearlie wasn't quiet."

Exactly, thought Jamie. Both the mention of "quiet" and "lamb" in relation to Pearlie made everything even funnier to Jamie. She wanted to hide her face, to shut out from her sight and hearing what was going on. Instead a snicker rose up in her, a catch of breath between an impulse to cry because she couldn't understand death and Pearlie Wu was dead, and a desire to laugh.

A furious red flushed Mrs. McClure's cheeks and she nailed Jamie with a slit-eyed look, but even her mean expression seemed comical.

Pearlie Wu's funeral was on now. Pearlie, who was never serious about anything, who teased everyone in town, was to be buried in the ground in that gray casket.

"Just as Pearlie Wu Graves was her husband's helpmate, selling the honey he harvested from his own beehives, she will no doubt be the Lord's handmaiden, dispensing honey in heaven," the minister said, his face pink as a ham.

Frederika fidgeted on the piano seat and Jamie felt another bubble of laughter coming up. She bent her head over, held her nose with one hand, and bit the knuckles of her other hand. She thought of trying to pass her mother in the row and escaping up the aisle and out of the building. Finally her laughter broke and caught.

The minister paused, and a terrible silence filled the room. His face was frozen with disapproval. Her mother's hand shot over and squeezed her knee sharply. "Stop giggling, Jamie. For heaven's sake, stop it," she whispered.

There was a faint rustle in the funeral chapel as others turned to stare. The minister resumed praising Pearlie and expressed astonishment that she had learned English in six months and had regular customers from all over the county at the stand in front of her house on Ashton Road.

Jamie hunched her shoulders while the minister talked about the mansions in God's house. She held on to her seat and squeezed it until her fingers turned white. When that didn't work, she bit the side of her mouth. She glanced up at the podium. Mr. Graves stared right at her. It was a downright murderous stare.

Hoo-boy, Jamie thought, quickly looking down at her lap. Her face straightened. Nothing, not one thing, was funny anymore.

"Lord, thou has been our refuge from generation to generation. Thou has set our misdeeds before thee," intoned the minister. He nodded at Frederika. Her stubby fingers played the first notes of "Amazing Grace."

Surely the service was almost over. Involuntarily Jamie looked at the door. Standing in the doorway was Zoe Warner. Her eyes were green, green as winter rye, and she gave Jamie a long green secret look. The light from the diamond-paned windows in the chapel lit her coppery hair that hung in springs down her back. Jamie thought Zoe had more hair than could possibly be on one head.

"That piano is really out of tune," a woman in front of them said to her husband.

Abruptly a muffled thumping came from within the piano. Frederika frowned fiercely. She played louder. This was not a good thing to do, because the piano instantly came alive with eerie yowls.

"What on earth?" asked Mrs. McClure.

Frederika's frowning features turned to wild-eyed panic. Still she played on. The parlor was full of bewildered faces and gasps. Mr. Jenner woke from a nap and muttered, "Turn that racket down."

A bone-blistering shriek followed by a guttural growl pierced the air.

Frederika covered her ears with her hands and scooted backward, upsetting the piano bench. She tumbled to the floor in a heap.

"For heaven's sake, man, finish up, finish up," Mr. Graves ordered the minister.

The minister raised his hands. "Please stay calm and remember that whatever is happening, it in no way interferes with our celebration of the life of Pearlie Wu Graves. Amen," he spluttered.

Jamie looked at Zoe. Her eyes were huge in her face. She stared at the proceedings with a baffled gaze.

A soft-spoken man whose hair was combed into a dark coppery mound stepped to the microphone. "I'm Mr. Warner, the funeral director. After paying your final respects, please assemble in your cars, and we will follow the Graves family to the graves…uh…cemetery, where a short ceremony will conclude the service."

The minister and Mr. Warner, tigerish looks in their eyes, strode to the piano. The minister slowly lifted the top. Lump popped his head out of the piano, crouching and looking as if he'd just been snatched from the jaws of death.

The mourners trailed in a line toward the casket, gawking and making sounds of surprise and outrage upon seeing a cat.

Mr. Jenner clicked his tongue. "Now how did that durn *cat* get in there?"

Mr. Warner reached for Lump, but Lump spit at him. He lost his nerve and stepped back, plowing into Frederika, who was bawling on the floor.

"Pearlie would have loved this," Jamie whispered to Gus. It was true. There was nothing her fun-loving friend had enjoyed so much as topsy-turvy situations. Gus looked thunderstruck and gripped Jamie's hand tight. He hung back for a moment when they reached the casket, but soon he peered into it.

Someone had made Pearlie's cheeks pink and her mouth bright red. Her face appeared waxy and was as white and pale as a turnip next to the pale silk casket pillow. Why was her dress so big? Was she expected to gain weight? Pearlie was *still*—that was the biggest difference. Not a muscle twitched.

Lump streaked behind them out the door. Jamie jerked Gus along until they were outside, where people stood in dazed clusters, blinking in the sunshine.

"What happened to the fur on the cat?" Gus asked, a tinge of hysteria in his voice.

"No one knows," Jamie said.

Her mother walked rapidly to the van that had TINKA'S CATERING on the side. A huge cake perched on top of it, complete with bride and groom.

Mrs. McClure stopped by the van door. "What is that on your neck?" she asked Jamie. "I thought it was a head you carried on that neck. What were you thinking of, laughing at a funeral? That woman was our neighbor, lived right next door for years. She was your good friend."

"Mother, I was so nervous," Jamie said. "The harder I tried not to, the harder it was."

Mrs. McClure shook her head. "That was the craziest service I've ever been to. They didn't need you laughing, and *that* was before the strange-looking cat."

"I feel just awful, Mother, I really do," Jamie said. "I loved Pearlie Wu." Her heart quickened and she felt tears forming behind her eyes. Some of the tears fell onto her cheeks. Gus immediately began snuffling.

Jamie thought she'd mastered the art of Never Crying in Public, No Matter What. Now she was crying, at the advanced age of twelve, on the sidewalk in front of Warner's Funeral Home while people got into their cars, including the blubbering Frederika Potts. Zoe Warner stood on the front porch with the same stunned look on her face.

"I'm going to the cemetery, and then I have to go to the grocery store. You and Gus walk straight home," Jamie's mother said.

The van door chunked shut, and her mother backed out and turned on University Avenue into the river of traffic, scattering birds over the Texas blue. The monstrous cake on top of the van rotated, as it always did when the van was in motion.

"I hate that cake on Mother's van," Jamie said. "It's so embarrassing." She wiped her cheeks with the backs of her hands.

Cars filed out of the lot with their lights on and moved slowly down the avenue toward the cemetery. Jamie felt the silent disapproval of the people inside the cars and imagined what they said to each other: It started, "Tinka McClure tries so hard," and ended, "You know, the father left the family years ago."

Chapter

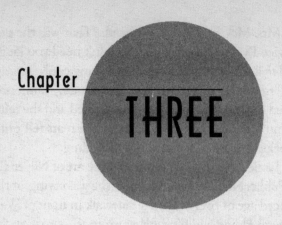

THREE

Jamie tried to stifle her tears, but they swam in her eyes and crowded her throat until it ached. Gus blubbered softly and took her hand. They followed the cars down University Avenue until the last one was out of sight. The streets of San Lucas were quiet now except for the sparrows screaming their heads off in the trees, their screaming making it all seem quieter.

"I loved Pearlie Wu, too," said Gus in a thin treble.

"I don't know what got into me," Jamie said, and sighed. "Remember when we made cards to sell?"

"Pearlie made most of them, but we got to keep the money." Tears crawled like insects down his face.

"My birthday!" Jamie said. "Pearlie always baked a honey cake and put sparklers on top instead of candles."

"Uh-huh," Gus said. "It had sesame seeds in it."

At that, Jamie felt a new batch of tears coming on, but she wanted Gus to quit crying.

Determined, she said, "When the going gets tough, the tough get going."

"Where do they go?" he asked.

"That's just a saying, Gus. It means we have to be strong. Pearlie would have wanted us to be strong."

Jamie looked down at Gus's six-year-old head. He was waist-high to her and his hair was gold, just like hers, the color of dandelions. Unlike hers, though, his hair was straight as a sheet and didn't wave and tangle. His skin was still a light tan from the summer.

They passed San Lucas University; Mrs. McClure catered receptions there. Students lounged on the grass, reading or sleeping. Across the street was the tall sandstone building that had TIMMONS COUNTY COURTHOUSE carved in an arch above the door. Surrounding the old courthouse was a square of shops and the Pig 'n' Whistle, where college students got barbecued pork sandwiches.

Two little boys on bicycles passed. "Hey, weenie brain!" one called to Gus as he whizzed by.

"Who are those kids?" Jamie asked.

Sighing, Gus waved a hand in the air as if to brush them away. "Eddie Potts. A fart. Luke Webb. Another fart." Gus whispered, "Sometimes they call me Baby Gussie."

"Why?"

"The first day of school the teacher told me my shoelace was untied at recess. Everyone watched me while I tried to tie it. I forgot how, and she had to tie it for me." Gus's bottom lip was out, making him look as if someone had smacked him.

"They're mean to you because of that?"

"I fall asleep, too." Gus's eyes were wide. "I saw the hyena in the yard a couple of nights ago."

"You did not," Jamie said.

"Did too," said Gus loudly as though Jamie were deaf,

23

his forehead wrinkling with emphasis. "It had a hunch-back and yellow eyes and striped fur."

"Gus," Jamie groaned.

"I couldn't sleep that whole night, and now I have bad dreams."

"I won't let it get you," Jamie promised.

"It could get you first and then get me."

Jamie shook her head. She was glad for a new topic, even if she'd been over this one again and again. She didn't want to think about Pearlie Wu and the funeral for a while.

"I didn't like first grade either," Jamie said. "The teacher always shushed everyone...Shh, shh, shh...all day long. And the boys were mean, too. I remember I hit a boy and the teacher kept me after school. I think his name was Davis Crockett. Anyway, he hated me because I could climb all the way up to the top of the slide the wrong way. You know, up the slide instead of the steps?"

"I can't do that." Gus looked dazzled.

"This Davis Crockett put sand on the slide to make it even more slippery, and I still did it. When I got to the top, I let out a war whoop. No boy could do it. He called me bad names, and I hit him."

"Do you have friends at your new school?" Gus asked. Even when his face was relaxed, he looked as though he had just heard something amazing.

"St. Agnes is different from public school," Jamie said. "The girls go around in the halls and at breaks in little groups. They've known each other all their lives. It's like turning on a complicated television show in the middle and trying to understand."

"You can still be friends with people from your old school, like Mary Lieta," Gus said. "Or you could have Jennifer over. I like Mary Lieta and Jennifer."

"Mary Lieta moved to Florida after school was out last year, and Jennifer lives in the country. She has a lot of chores. I really miss them. They were my best friends."

What Jamie thought but couldn't say out loud for fear of crying was: I told all my real secrets to Pearlie. Now she's gone, too.

"I'm friends with Jeffrey Dengler," Gus said, his gray eyes wide. "He found dog biscuits in his desk last week."

"I have a new plan," Jamie said. "At first I was mad at Mother for putting me in St. Agnes. She thinks I'm getting a better education in private school. But I'm not mad at her anymore. I'm going to go to classes and just keep to myself. My grades will be great because I don't have anyone to talk to. A lot of grownups live their whole lives that way."

Even as she said it, it sounded lonely and terrible. She felt as hollow as a blown egg when she thought of having no one to spend time with or laugh with.

Gus frowned. From his pants pocket he pulled two flat bubblegums wrapped with baseball cards inside and gave her one. They walked in silence for a long while.

In the golden light of late afternoon they finally turned off University Avenue onto Ashton Road. The gaslights on the paved streets across University to the east of Ashton would soon light up. Houses on that side of the wide avenue were old and "stately," as Mrs. McClure said. Most of the St. Agnes girls lived on those streets.

Directly south of Ashton Road was Daffodil Lane, and just after that was the entrance to the old San Lucas

Memorial Cemetery. It was the section of town tagged Booger Hollow because it was close to the cemetery. Some of the old-timers in San Lucas claimed to have seen ghosts in the neighborhood and declared it Booger Holler.

Gus found a hop toad and urged it up the hill by gently poking it with a stick. "Why do they give dead people pillows?"

"I don't know," Jamie said.

"Is Pearlie a booger now?"

"Ghost, Gus. Booger is a trashy word for ghost."

"Well, is she a booger?" Gus persisted. "Will she be hanging around Booger Hollow now?"

"No, she's an angel in heaven. And don't even think about it. Between Sasquatches and hyenas, there are too many bad fears in your head already. There's no room for any more fears, Gus."

Thick chinaberry trees hung out over either side of the road. When clouds passed over the sun, the leaves darkened and made the road seem like a shadowy tunnel.

Once they topped the hill, Gus scampered ahead, his body mottled by light and leaf shadow. The seven houses on Ashton Road were built on the north side; across the street were fields of alfalfa and clover. There were three big rock houses. Jamie and Gus were the only children on the block, and they lived in one of the three white clapboards with wraparound porches. The smaller rock house that Pearlie Wu had lived in with Mr. Graves was next door at the end of the road.

Gus suddenly burst out laughing. "Look at Tank," he yelled back over his shoulder, pointing at their big boxer.

Tank trudged across Ashton Road. Suspended from his mouth was a large waffle. He stopped, surveyed the field for spies, and carefully put the waffle down. Dirt flew everywhere as he dug a hole beside it.

Tank was the only dog on the road. It was his afternoon routine to visit every house where he was welcome. He accepted the neighbors' offerings and buried everything that wasn't a favorite in the fields.

Gus jumped into one of the high-backed rockers on their front porch and squatted on the seat frog-fashion.

"Can I sleep in your room tonight?" he asked.

"You sleep in my room almost every night," Jamie said.

"It's because of having to live in Booger Hollow." Gus's eyes darkened.

"I like Booger Hollow," Jamie said. "Think of all the stories and legends about this neighborhood."

"Scary stories," Gus said. "Like that one about Joshua Wiggins. I think he looked in our window last night."

Joshua Wiggins was a child ghost Pearlie had told them about.

"Don't look like that, Gus. Nothing is going to hurt you, especially not a dead boy. Those stories are just for fun. They're make-believe. Besides, it's Friday. Let's try to be a little bit happy about *that*."

To take his mind off his fears, she lifted Gus up in a roughhouse way and sang into his face, "Gus the muss makes a terrible fuss, but JAMIE'S NOT SCARED OF ANYTHING!"

And because he was light, she carried him giggling through the back door into the kitchen. They ate bowls of cereal and pieces of buttered toast for dinner, their bare heels hooked on the rungs of their chairs and their elbows on the table.

Evening shadows closed over the big kitchen when Tank whined at the back door. Jamie went to the pantry and filled his bowl with food. When she carried it out the back door, Tank and Gus were on the patio. The big boxer's mouth was full of bubblegum. He chewed it awkwardly, his head and neck snapping so that he looked as if he were trying to spit out a snake.

"That's too much sugar for Tank, Gus. It's bad for his teeth and he's too fat already."

Gus kissed Tank on the lips. "Tank loves bubblegum. I think if he saw the hyenas he would bark," Gus said.

Tank swallowed most of the gum and attacked the dog food, making lapping and smacking noises. Gus petted him while he ate.

Jamie heard the van before she saw it. Usually she could figure out from the way her mother pulled in from work what kind of mood she was in. If she was hassled or in a hurry, Mrs. McClure raced headlong for the end of the drive, slamming on the brakes just short of the garage. Other days the van came in at a sad, slow creep. This was the moment Jamie had dreaded, and she wasn't surprised when the van roared in and lurched to a halt.

Her mother got out with grocery bags in her arms. Tank bounded toward her and jumped on her legs. Mrs. McClure stumbled backward, dropping one of the bags. The brown bag burst, and apples, oranges, pears, and plums rolled across the patio.

Gus ran over and grabbed Tank's collar. Jamie pulled her skirt up, making a sack of it, and darted about, gathering up the rolling fruit.

Mrs. McClure looked pinched, as though someone had been squeezing her all day. She jittered her foot, which was clad in a black shiny leather pump, against the patio.

"That fruit is for the compotes for Mrs. Atwell's luncheon tomorrow. If it's bruised, I'll have to go back to the store." She took a deep breath, followed by a long pause, as if, attempting to control her temper, she was counting to ten.

"Jamie, come in now. We need to talk."

Mrs. McClure flipped on the kitchen light with her free hand. The large kitchen had several ovens and stove tops. There were long counters with metal racks overhead where countless pots and pans, shiny and clean, hung. The room was always spotless because it was headquarters for her catering service, and it had to pass health inspections at a moment's notice.

Mrs. McClure put the bags down on a counter and took Jamie's face in her hands. She searched Jamie's face with the same puzzled expression she might give to one of her soufflés, her time-tested chocolate soufflé, for instance, when, one time in one hundred, it fell.

"I don't know what happened to you this afternoon," she began, "but laughter at a funeral is inappropriate. We cannot be the cause of anything hurtful to Mr. Graves and his sister with all they're going through."

Shame ran through Jamie like a sword. She'd tried to put off thinking about Pearlie's funeral as long as possible.

Mrs. McClure's right eyelid twittered. "I've been thinking about how to begin to make things right, and this is what I've decided. I want you to take an angel food cake—I have one on hand—over to them now. It will be a sympathy call, but I also want you to tell them how sorry you are, that it was your first funeral, and that it was nerves that caused you to behave as you did."

Jamie felt panic rise in her. She blurted, "I can't! It's too soon, and I don't even know Mr. Graves except to wave at. He's a hermit. You know Pearlie always said he was a hermit, Mother. Besides, they won't want company now."

"Mr. Graves is very involved with his bees, Jamie. It doesn't mean he doesn't have feelings."

Jamie was desperate. "You've never really talked to him either, and we've lived here since Gus was a baby."

Mrs. McClure abruptly folded her arms across her chest. If she'd been at the North Pole, her voice couldn't have been colder. "You will go. You will take the cake. You will sit down and talk with Mr. Graves and his sister."

Jamie knew she could try to change her mother's mind, but it would be impossible. Mrs. McClure would stand in the kitchen like a salt block, with that face that meant business, all night if she had to. For the rest of Jamie's life, if necessary.

There was a weariness around Mrs. McClure's mouth when she handed Jamie the plate with the big white cake on it.

Straightening, Mrs. McClure flipped back her hair in a familiar gesture—efficient, back to her usual business of organizing. "Hike now," she said.

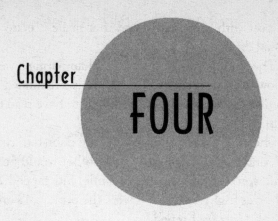

Chapter FOUR

It was dark and Jamie walked slowly down the drive and across the yard, muttering under her breath. How had she let herself get into this mess anyway? Why couldn't she back up and start the whole day over?

Jamie stumbled over Gus's soccer ball and almost dropped the cake. She angrily kicked the ball across the yard.

The creamy moon was full and rising. Everything was silent except for the chirp of crickets and the foamy toss of the wind in the trees.

The sight of the honey stand by the Graves's gate wrenched her heart. The armless rocker that Pearlie sat in was still there, in front of the brown picket fence surrounding the front yard. Jamie frowned, trying to call up Pearlie's laughing face, her small hands, slender neck, and the gleam of straight black hair cut like Joan of Arc's with bangs.

Pearlie's wooden sign—HONEY FOR SALE—hung from a broken chain, and the wind knocked it against the post with a muffled sound that made it echo like a funeral drum.

The front porch light was on, illuminating a yard full of flowers in neat beds. The little house reminded Jamie of a picture in a book you'd be happy to have read to you again and again.

She could leave the cake on the doorstep, ring the bell, and run, but she knew her mother would find out. Jamie forced her face into a smile and rapped twice, feeling as frightened as if it were the principal's office at school. *More* frightened.

Miss Graves answered the door with a puzzled expression. Jamie couldn't think of a thing to say.

"I brought you a cake," she finally said, unnecessary as that was.

Miss Graves opened the screen door. "Come in," she said with gentle politeness. She took the cake, and rustling in her dark dress like an old crow, she led Jamie to an old-fashioned claw-footed sofa in the living room.

"Teddy," she called into the hall. "Someone is here to see you." Lamplight fell across her thin face, highlighting its wrinkles and folds. She was old. Her powdered face had a streak on it where tears had run into the hair at her temples and dried.

Jamie had always thought of Pearlie, even though she was quick and young at heart, as old. And though she only had a waving relationship with Mr. Graves, she thought he was old as well. But he was strong. She'd watched him from her bedroom window doing jumping jacks and push-ups on his back porch in the morning.

Mr. Graves appeared in the doorway in white shirt

sleeves, collar open, showing gray chest hairs. His blue eyes were dark-ringed with exhaustion in his weather-beaten face, and he had a trimmed gray beard. She'd never seen him this close before.

Jamie jumped up and clasped both hands behind her back, where each controlled the other's trembling.

"Ah, there you are," Miss Graves said. "The little neighbor girl brought a nice cake. I'll just take it to the kitchen." She shuffled out of the room.

Mr. Graves took a step toward her, and she took a step back, into the sofa, and sat down hard. The impact must have jarred something loose inside her because she started to talk.

"I came to say that I'm so sorry for your trouble, Mr. Graves, for what happened to Pearlie and all."

Mr. Graves sat down in the love seat and dropped his hands between his knees. His knuckles were the size of walnuts.

"I hope you didn't mind me being around the honey stand so much with my little brother."

He turned his square, ruddy face toward her. "You were on the porch with Pearlie just last week. All that drawing and paper folding..."

"Christmas cards," Jamie said. "My mother works pretty hard most of the time. Pearlie was always outside and..."

"I know all about you," Mr. Graves interrupted. "Pearlie liked children more than adults. She talked about you and your little brother at dinner." He looked at the ceiling. "Let's see. You hate being tall for your age, and you slump to disguise it. You changed to St. Agnes

Hall this year. It's an all-girls school. Pearlie said you'd taken to calling it St. Agonies because you're lonely and unhappy there."

Jamie was shocked. Pearlie told her secret feelings at the dinner table?

"I'm not lonely," she protested, her voice squeaky and sissy sounding, but she couldn't help it.

A big orange cat with a tattered ear jumped on Mr. Graves's lap and he stroked it. "Your little brother is scared of his own shadow. Pearlie thought he needed a father or someone to chase the fears from his mind and protect him. You try to do it because your mother is too busy cooking, trying to make ends meet."

Jamie's mouth moved before she could even give it permission. "What else did Pearlie say about us?"

"Your father didn't like being an associate professor. When the university didn't make him a full professor, he moved and took a job at a school in Tucson, I think. Your brother was very young then, and your mother was tired of moving around. She'd started her catering business."

Jamie sat still as a statue, her hand gripping the mahogany claws of the sofa. She had a sore tooth. Out of habit she pressed on it with her tongue, knowing it would hurt. She felt the same desire to encourage Mr. Graves to go on.

"Did she say anything else?"

Mr. Graves hesitated. "Your father has a new wife and baby," he went on. "He doesn't call as much anymore, much less invite you or or your brother out to visit. A card now and then, or a package on your birthday."

Telling Jamie's secrets put some color back in Mr. Graves's face. Jamie felt peculiar meeting his eyes, so she just stared past his head. What a weird way to behave on the night of his wife's funeral. Jamie remembered her own weird behavior and thought of the sequence of events that led to this moment. He was trying to hurt her because she had laughed at the funeral.

"I didn't mean to laugh today," she said. "It was all so hard to believe, and I know it was a terrible thing to do. It's just that I was really nervous. I hope I didn't ruin the funeral. When Reverend Burger called her 'quiet' and a 'lamb,' I just…" Jamie held her palms up as if she were surrendering under fire.

Mr. Graves looked down at the cat in his lap. "Tell me, Jamie, how did you get that bizarre-looking cat in the piano?"

Jamie's breath caught. "You think *I* put Lump in that piano?"

"Why not? You seem to have an odd sense of humor." The orange cat purred like a refrigerator in the middle of the night, a sound Jamie wouldn't have noticed if the conversation had continued. Jamie wanted to get away. Mr. Graves was a strange man. No wonder Pearlie never took anyone beyond the front door.

"Mr. Graves, I loved Pearlie." Tears stung Jamie's eyes. "I don't know what happened to me today, but I didn't put the cat in the piano. I would never have done that."

Mr. Graves merely looked down at the orange cat in his lap.

"I ought to go now. I need to get on home," she said, and stood up. "Tell your sister good-bye for me. I'm going now," she said on her way to the door. She let herself out without even looking back.

Once out of the Graves's yard, Jamie ran toward the bright squares of light in the windows that were home. She heard the familiar sound of Gus and her mother calling to each other across the house when she went in the front door.

She ran upstairs, then up another short flight of stairs to her bedroom. It had been an attic full of old trunks, newspapers, and dozens of department-store boxes before her mother had it converted to a slanty-ceilinged bedroom for her.

Jamie took off her clothes, crumpled them into a ball, and pulled on a nightgown. Usually her bedroom cheered her up. It was like a tree house—a kind of lookout. Each side of the room had a window with a window seat. She could see what was happening on Ashton Road from the front window and what was going on in Pearlie's backyard from the back window.

Tonight the room bothered her. It was too busy. The big iron bed that was painted the color of eggshells seemed bright. Her quilt had every color of the rainbow, and on the floor was a yellow braided rug.

She pulled *The Pigman*, her new library book, from her backpack and tried reading it for a while. When tears fell on the page, she sat on the edge of her bed, shoulders slumped, elbows resting on her knees, stomach twisted like a cat's cradle.

The floorboards creaked. Her mother sat next to Jamie on the bed and put her cheek next to hers. "Are you okay?"

Jamie hoped her mother would whisper a secret, some way to forget the day and get through the lonely weeks ahead at school. She had always been able to look right into Jamie's heart.

Jamie crumpled against her mother's chest and sobbed.

"It was awful. Pearlie won't ever be back again. And I tried to apologize," she said between sobs. "I guess Pearlie needed something to talk to him about at the dinner table. She told him all this stuff about our family, how many problems we've had and all."

"Why, I think we get by just fine," Mrs. McClure said, patting Jamie's back. "We've had our troubles, but I've got more business than I can handle now. You're at a fine new school, and Gus will grow out of his fears."

"It's the way he said it—kind of mean."

"Mr. Graves isn't mean, Jamie. He's just eccentric. Now that Pearlie is gone, he must be feeling scared and angry. I think he's going to need people."

Jamie was seized by a spasm of guilt. "And the way I behaved today. I'll just never understand it."

Mrs. McClure took Jamie's shoulders and looked at her. "You just tell yourself, 'That wasn't like me. I won't do it again.' Apologizing to him was the right thing to do. You can go to sleep with a clear conscience."

"Mother, he thinks I put Lump in the piano."

"Lump?"

"That's the name of the cat at Pearlie's funeral. Lump lives at St. Agnes."

"How odd!"

"No kidding it's odd." Jamie's voice rose. "Lump

didn't just stroll over to the funeral home and jump into the piano. He's too old and fat to do it if he wanted to. Someone had to put him there. I told you that school is weird."

"Oh, Jamie. Don't start that again."

"Mother, those girls do the craziest things. I never know what's going to happen from one minute to the next. I mean it." She felt her stomach loosen a little. "Some of it's pretty funny, though," she said more to herself than to her mother.

"It's a good school, Jamie. The best. The girls are smart, and they come from good families. You're getting a better education. You have to trust me on this."

Jamie hung her head. She heard Gus walk up to the bed. His sticky hand touched the back of her bent neck with tiny pats.

"Just remember, honey," her mother said. "Even a spotted pig looks black at night."

"What's that supposed to mean?" Jamie looked up.

"Things always look better in the morning."

"I don't want to sleep in my room tonight," Gus whined.

"Can he sleep in here?" Mrs. McClure asked. "I have all that food to make. I don't have time to keep putting him back in his own bed."

"I can't even be alone when I sleep, Mother! He's even moved his little turtle into my room. It smells like turtle food in here now."

Gus whimpered into the silence.

"Oh, all right," Jamie said. "Come on, Gus."

Gus plugged his elephant night-light into the wall.

It cast a blue light in the corner of the bedroom, which annoyed Jamie, but she pulled the covers back and he crawled into bed.

Mrs. McClure flipped off the light and turned on the ceiling fan over the bed. She left the room.

"Spotted pigs," Jamie muttered. She pulled the covers up.

Down the road there was a cat fight. The willow tree outside Jamie's window made leaf patterns that moved gently on the wall.

"I know there are Sasquatches," Gus suddenly whispered into her face. "I figured out why."

"I told you there weren't, Gus." Jamie was tired. The day suddenly seemed a week long.

"They smell terrible," Gus said. "If they were make-believe, how could they smell so bad? If something smells bad, it has to *be*, right?"

"Not necessarily. Maybe that's just part of the legend. Besides, even if there are, no one has ever seen or smelled a Sasquatch in Texas. No Sasquatches in Texas," she said firmly. Sometimes it helped to tell Gus something twice.

Gus moved closer and yawned. "Tell me the story of where we're from again."

Jamie's resentment was too slippery to hold. She put her arm over Gus. She would hold him and try to protect him from the meanness of first grade, the reality of not having a father nearby.

"We come from Shangri-la," she whispered into his hair. She loved the way the word sounded. "Our father was the ruler of Shangri-la, and everyone loved him. We lived in a palace made of crystals, and it was surrounded

39

by guards. Their faces were painted red and green and blue. These guards were everywhere, and when we went outside, they followed us to be sure we were safe."

Already Gus was asleep. She heard him breathing in the darkness. He lay pale and small in the moonlight, a salty boy-smell about him. Downstairs a pot lid clanked. Her mother would cook late into the night.

Her mind looped around and around as it replayed the events of the day; Mr. Hughes-Walter's padlock, the funeral, Lump's screeching in the piano. How did he get there? Why would someone from St. Agnes sneak Lump over and put him there on purpose? Kai painted Mr. Hughes-Walter's padlock just a few hours before, but Zoe looked completely stunned when Lump started shrieking. Wouldn't Zoe know if Kai was pulling another prank?

Zoe Warner's smile flashed in and out of her consciousness. It always came back to that; every train of memory twisted on its track and returned to the girl with the green eyes and springy hair. Zoe's secret smile was the only good thing that had happened that day.

Chapter 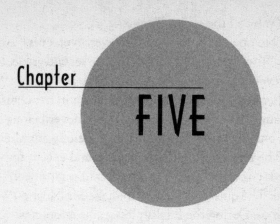 FIVE

The news of Lump's appearance at Pearlie's funeral went through St. Agnes like fire in dry grass. Stories rustled up and down the halls on Monday. Jamie was itching with curiosity. She didn't want to ask Theresa any more questions, but who else was there to ask?

Jamie took a deep breath and turned to Theresa before the bell rang. "Would you please tell me what's going on around here? Do you know anything about Lump?"

"What about Lump?" Theresa asked. She glanced across the aisle at Abigail, whose eyes narrowed.

"Well, for starters, how did he get that Mohawk?" Jamie asked.

"I told you last week I don't know anything about that," Theresa said.

Jamie decided to persist. "Well, how did he get in the piano at the funeral?"

"I don't know," Theresa said, crossing her heart with her finger. "I swear I don't."

"Even if she did, she couldn't tell you," Abigail quickly added.

"Why all the secrets?"

"No one rats at St. Agnes. Never, ever, ever," Abigail said. "You learn that somehow by the second grade. If you rat, everyone makes your life miserable."

Jamie turned around and sank down in her chair. Her life already *was* miserable. She would never belong here. Not only that, she'd probably never belong anywhere.

The air was close that morning, and except for whispered conversations, the classroom was quieter than usual. The quietness seemed to make Mr. Hughes-Walter nervous. During the English lesson, he wrote new vocabulary words on the chalkboard. He whirled around from time to time as though he felt sure to catch one of the girls creeping up behind him with a snake.

"It's a pretty day," he finally said just before lunch. "I think we'll eat outside and take a long break in the courtyard."

Jamie groaned inwardly. She liked to eat in the cafeteria. They had assigned seats, so there was no question of feeling awkward or being alone.

She sat on a low wall in the sunshine and ate her sandwich while reading *The Pigman*, which was about two high school kids who felt out of things too.

At the end of a chapter Jamie looked up. Zoe stooped in the courtyard to tie a small girl's shoelaces. A few feet away Kai shook her head at the twins as if they were hopeless, while they collapsed in giggles. Soon all four heads tilted together and they talked quietly. Jamie felt the familiar tug of loneliness, shut her book, and slid down from the wall. She headed inside for the bathroom as Abigail Frank approached the group.

Jamie went into the first stall, locked the door, and put the toilet seat cover down. She sat on it and put her feet up on the locked door. She opened her book to read again. This had become her custom when she was uncomfortable at school and wanted to get away for a few minutes.

Someone came in, washed her hands, and left. Jamie was just feeling calm when the door opened again.

"Merit," Kai's hoarse voice whispered harshly, "see if anyone is here."

Jamie went rigid as Merit tried the door and walked up and down in front of the stalls.

"The first one is locked, but there's no one in it," Merit finally said. "It's all clear."

Jamie's face felt like a furnace. She had a moment's notion to call out, but instead she sat there, tense, breathing steadily and quietly and just a little fast. Through trial and error she'd chosen this stall because there was a crack in the wood on the side. She could see through it so that if a teacher came in she could put her feet down or leave.

Merit and Vivica stood on either side of Zoe and Kai. Abigail Frank faced them with her back to the sink.

"Now, what did you say you did?" A cold fire was behind Zoe's green eyes.

"I was the one who put Lump in the piano," Abigail said, her voice pinched with secrecy.

"Why did you do it?" Kai asked.

Abigail faced their anger with an intense gaze. "I know what's going on. At least I think I do," she finally said. "You're starting the circle again, and I want to be part of it."

"You don't have any proof," Merit said.

"No," Abigail said, "but all the signs are there. Who else would have done those pranks the first few days. of school? Kai painted Mr. Hughes-Walter's lock black in front of everyone, and I know *I* didn't give Lump the Mohawk."

"Maybe we're starting the circle and maybe we aren't," Kai said crossly. "Even if we were, you'd have to be asked first, Abigail. You can't just haul off and decide to do any old thing and *then* be asked."

"You have to admit," Vivica said, "she didn't exactly call and ask for Prince Albert in a can. That stunt at the funeral took guts."

"My father is embarrassed about what happened at the funeral," Zoe said to Vivica. "We would never have someone do that."

"I have as much right to be part of the circle as you do," Abigail said to Kai in a shaking voice. "Our big sisters started it up together when they were at St. Agnes. I just thought…"

"Yeah, Abigail," Kai interrupted, "and who told your *mother* all about it and whose mother told Miss Pickney?"

"Well," Abigail said, "my sister *had* to tell my mother. What was she supposed to do when the nuns found her in the Our Lady of Sorrows confessional booth in her underwear?"

"She squealed, Abigail," Kai said, hands on her hips, "so that gives you no rights, period. The school doesn't approve of the circle. If they even *think* someone is starting it again, they'll be watching us all like hawks. You

44

also have no proof that I've been doing anything other than having a little fun with Pukes-Walter."

"You may have gotten us in trouble, too, Abigail," Merit said.

"How could I get you in trouble?"

"Think about it. Lump lives at St. Agnes," Merit said. "Miss Pickney isn't senile. She'll know someone from St. Agnes put him in the piano when she hears about the funeral."

"I'm sure she's already heard," Vivica said. "Who hasn't?"

"She might think one of us did it," Kai said. "Mouths were working overtime in the halls this morning."

"You need to confess, Abigail," Merit said. "We don't want to get blamed for something we didn't do."

"No!" Abigail exploded. "I can't! I mean, think about it. It's not like me to cause trouble. They'd want to know why I did it."

"She's right," Kai said to the others. She gave Abigail her best you-are-so-annoying expression. "If one of us gets called in about this, Abigail, you'll really be sorry. I promise you that."

Abigail chewed a nail. "If something like that happens, we could sort of imply to Miss Pickney that it was that new girl, Jamie."

Jamie flinched and blurted, "Don't you dare! I'm not taking the blame for Lump being at Pearlie's funeral."

She popped up from her seat on the commode lid, unlocked the stall door, and came out. Her anger made her forget she was eavesdropping.

"What are you doing in here?" Kai asked, looking astonished for a change.

"I was reading, that's all," Jamie said.

"No way," Merit said. "There weren't any feet under that stall."

"Well," Jamie responded, "I propped them up on the door and you surprised me. I didn't have time to say anything."

"Oh, right," Kai said sarcastically. She turned to Abigail. "This is a mess, Abigail. Do you see what you've done? Now someone else is involved."

Abigail colored and frowned so hard her mouth bent into the shape of a horseshoe.

Kai glared at Jamie. "No one would have put the blame on you anyway. We don't rat at St. Agnes."

"Okay," Jamie murmured. She tried to squeeze by, but Kai blocked her way.

"Where are you going?" Kai asked.

"I think I'm late," Jamie said.

"You're going to be later." Kai pointed her forefinger at Jamie like a pistol. "I repeat, we do not rat on each other at St. Agnes. Even if you can't stand the sight of someone, you don't do or say anything that will get them in trouble."

"I wouldn't," Jamie said, trying to squeeze by Kai.

"One more thing," Kai commanded. "Forget everything you heard in here. *Everything*."

"I've already forgotten," Jamie said.

"Promise," Kai ordered.

Jamie turned her palms up. "I promise." Should I salute, too? she wondered.

"So we'll just keep a tight lid on all this and no one will get in trouble," Kai said in a warning tone. She turned to the mirror and ran a hand quickly through her hair as if that settled that.

After school, Jamie felt even more questions stack up in her forehead. What exactly was this circle Abigail was talking about, and why would she do something as extreme as putting Lump in the piano?

Why was Kai so determined to keep it all a secret if there wasn't anything more going on than a few practical jokes?

As she leaned out her bedroom window and idly watched Mr. Graves work in his bee yard, Jamie got so lost in these questions that she sat there until the sun was completely gone.

She was startled to attention when Mr. Graves turned on a flashlight. He shone the light at the opening of each hive, his head bent close to the entrance. He cupped his hand between his mouth and the hole in the exact manner of a person whispering a secret into another's ear.

Jamie drew back from the window and stood up straight. What was this? Just as she'd stumbled onto the conversation in the bathroom earlier in the day, Jamie had a vague sense of intruding, of seeing something meant to be private.

"What's outside?" Gus whispered loudly.

Jamie jumped. She hadn't even heard her brother approach. "Gus, you scared me to death!" she exclaimed.

"Why are you standing in the dark?" he persisted. "What's out there?"

"I can't figure out what Mr. Graves is doing. He's talking to the bees or something."

Gus watched for a long while, frowning, one bare foot on top of the other. Jamie's whole body was taut with alertness. She thought she could almost hear grass blades touching out in the bee yard.

"He's going to get stung sticking his head up to the hole like that," Gus finally said.

In a twinkling she heard herself say in a voice suddenly firm, "You stay here and watch me from the window. I'm going to sneak over there and see if I can find out what he's doing."

"I'm not staying in the house by myself," Gus protested.

"Well, Mother won't be back for at least an hour. You don't like to be outside at night."

"You can't leave me," Gus whined. "I'll be scared."

"If you go with me, you'll still be scared."

"You can't go either, Jamie." Gus's chin quivered.

"I'm going," Jamie said.

"Jamieeeee." Tears welled up in Gus's eyes.

"Oh, come on, then," Jamie said. She narrowed her eyes into spying slits. "Pretend you're a secret agent and you're going into enemy territory. You have to be quiet."

In moments they were outside. Jamie chained Tank to the fence so he wouldn't follow them and took Gus's hand.

They padded through the yard in the moonlight, shadows running long and short ahead of them. The tree swing creaked gently, causing Gus to hop sideways into Jamie.

"Shh," she said, and carefully pushed her way through the privet hedge to Mr. Graves's backyard.

They crept to the large magnolia tree on the far side of the honey house. Jamie pressed her back to the tree and held Gus against her in the dark. Now take yourself right back home, she said in her mind, but she was unable to obey her own order.

Mr. Graves's voice, low and urgent, drifted across the yard. Jamie crouched to her knees and peered around the tree trunk. He was several feet away and had come to the end of a row of beehives. He lifted his head, straightened his shoulders, and went to the next hive.

"Pearlie is dead," he said. "There's nothing to be done about it. Pearlie is dead."

He repeated this again and again, so that it finally seemed as if the words were coming out of the boxes. Jamie felt the hair on the back of her neck move, and a chill went up her spine.

"Jamie, puhleeze!" Gus whispered. "Can we get out of here?"

Jamie ignored him.

Mr. Graves tied something to the hive. When he moved away, a scrap of dark cloth fluttered in the breeze like a flag.

Tank barked across the yard. Shadowy headlights shone through the hedges, and the faint sound of wheels crunching gravel caused Jamie to take Gus's hand and creep back through the privet hedge.

Chapter

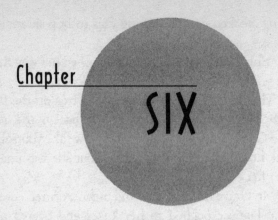

SIX

Jamie's stomach flipped when she saw her mother's van in the driveway. When they went into the kitchen, Gus's face had the flushed look it always had when he was getting ready to spill the beans.

"Guess what!" Gus said loudly.

"What?" Mrs. McClure asked.

"Mr. Graves is over there telling his bees that Pearlie Wu is dead!" Gus said.

"Have you two been spying on Mr. Graves?" Mrs. McClure asked. She tied an apron on.

"Not really," Jamie said. She glanced down at Gus. "Well, maybe."

"Jamie McClure! After everything that poor man has been through," Mrs. McClure said. "There's nothing worse than morbid curiosity."

"He didn't see us. Mother, he's actually out there putting his mouth up to every hive, telling those bees what happened to Pearlie," Jamie said.

"He has to," Mrs. McClure said. She took another apron off a hook and handed it to Jamie. "They could consider themselves neglected and take it into their minds to leave if he didn't."

"Bees don't know stuff like that," Gus said. "They're insects."

"I went to the country every summer when I was a child," Mrs. McClure said. "I knew a couple of beekeepers. They were very superstitious about their hives. If someone was born or someone died, they always told the bees. They made a regular ceremony out of it."

"It's still creepy," Jamie said.

"No more snooping, you two," her mother said, signaling the conversation was over. "Now, help me mix a batch of batter for strawberry shortcake. My new ulcers have a hard day to look forward to tomorrow. I need some help."

The hot weather intensified, making Jamie want to jump out of her skin. All week a cloud of anticipation hung over the class, as if everyone was waiting for the next move. Miss Pickney never called anyone from the class to her office, but Abigail Frank stared at Jamie from time to time with the trace of a warning in her tight pale face.

Just after lunch period toward the end of the week, Mr. Hughes-Walter yanked down a pink and blue and yellow wall map of the world. It rolled right back up. He took a deep breath and pulled it down again slowly. He still seemed tense when he had to stand with his back to the room.

A balled-up piece of notebook paper hit Jamie's arm. She looked around and met Zoe's eyes. Zoe pointed briefly to the floor, then turned back to look at Mr. Hughes-Walter.

"Open your geography books to page twenty," he said, an edge to his voice.

Jamie vaguely heard him, but she picked up the wad of paper instead. She quietly opened it.

> Dear Jamie,
> What you did at the funeral last Friday? When you laughed? Don't feel too bad. It happens sometimes. I ought to know.
>
> Zoe
>
> P.S. That map looks like someone got sick on it.

The room was so still that all Jamie heard was the whirring of cicadas in the oak trees outside.

She felt a keen stab of pleasure and looked at Zoe. But Zoe stared hard at her geography book. Jamie glanced around. Kids were looking at her. Mr. Hughes-Walter made a little sniffing sound. He was standing in front of her desk and held out his hand for the note.

Jamie reluctantly gave Zoe's note to Mr. Hughes-Walter, and he read it to himself.

He looked from Jamie to Zoe. "I've had it," he said in a disgusted tone. "I have really just had it. You girls take this note and your things to Miss Pickney's office now. This second."

Zoe's chair scraped back. Jamie grabbed her backpack and got up quietly, her heart loud in her chest. She'd never been to a principal's office.

"I don't even know where Miss Pickney's office is," she said softly, turning back to look at Mr. Hughes-Walter.

"Come on," said Zoe. "I know."

Once in the hall, Jamie walked in silence beside Zoe. "I don't get it," she finally said. "A lot of other things are going on—what with the white mice and the earthworms and his old padlock—why would he send us to the office just because of a note?"

Zoe smiled at Jamie sideways. "Culprits. Remember? Things have happened, but this is the first time he's caught anyone. Anyway, don't worry about it. If we're lucky and she's busy, geography may be over by the time we get back to class."

They walked outside and through the gargoyle-festooned entrance to the small house on the side of the school that was Miss Pickney's office. Dread seeped through Jamie. What if she cried?

"Hmm?" The secretary looked up.

"Zoe Warner and Jamie McClure to see Miss Pickney, please." Zoe's clear green gaze was level and calm.

"Miss Pickney is in meetings this afternoon," the secretary said. "What's this about?"

"A note that Mr. Hughes-Walter found," Zoe said.

"So it's disciplinary?"

Zoe shrugged. "I guess."

"Well, in that case," the secretary said, "wait at the picnic table out front. She'll have to work you in between meetings. Let me have the note."

Once outside, Jamie said, "You aren't even nervous, are you?"

Zoe stared at the old pink brick building. The

wrought-iron balconies were covered with fig ivy. "I've been at St. Agnes since preschool. By now I guess I know what to be nervous about. It's not Miss Pickney."

They sat down on a picnic bench beneath a ring of pecan trees. Overhead the trees leaned together, then apart, making whispery noises in the wind. Jamie really looked at Zoe. She was small and old-fashioned looking. She reminded Jamie of a girl in an old photograph.

Zoe looked up at the trees. "Those noisy trees remind me of a game we used to play. Gossip? Did you ever play that?" Zoe asked.

"Oh," Jamie answered, remembering. "The one where you sat in a circle and whispered a message to the kid next to you? You'd start out with, say, 'Sandy's family is really poor,' and end up with 'Grandpa has rocks in his underwear drawer.'"

"That's it," Zoe said. "Everyone laughed so hard."

"Well, everyone but Sandy," Jamie said.

"Yeah," Zoe said softly.

"Can I ask you something?"

"Ask away."

"Does that really happen at funerals? I mean, other people laugh, too?" Jamie asked.

"Sometimes," Zoe said. "The worst time was when this woman came in from out of town for a relative's funeral. She stood up and hollered, 'God's pee-pee!' I slip into the funerals when I don't have anything else to do. They really make some people nervous."

"No kidding," Jamie said. "But at least that woman didn't live in San Lucas."

"Well, true." Zoe thought a moment. "About a month

ago old man Friar fell asleep and snored really loud during Mrs. Pope's service. She was a teacher, and some of her third graders were there. One giggled, then another one, and pretty soon they all did. It was like a virus, contagious or something."

Jamie stared ahead. "I was so afraid I'd laugh. It was nerves. I thought, 'If I can think it, I can do it.' And then I did. I can't stop thinking about how awful it was."

Zoe's face softened. "She was a really good friend, huh?"

"Pearlie let my little brother and me help at her honey stand. We poured honey into jars and put the labels on. We decorated the jars for Halloween, Thanksgiving, Christmas—really, all the holidays. We've been going over to her stand since Gus was three," Jamie explained. "My mother was furious at me after the funeral."

Zoe nodded. Understanding glimmered on her face.

"I had to apologize to Mr. Graves," Jamie continued. She felt a lightness ripple through her body. It was good to talk to someone about the last few days.

"Was he angry?" Zoe asked.

"He was strange and kind of mean," Jamie said. "My mother thinks he's scared now that Pearlie's gone."

Jamie decided to change the subject. "Do you live above the funeral home?"

"Yep." Zoe nodded.

"What's it like?"

"I don't know any different," Zoe said. "I've lived there all my life. And my father's always lived there and even my grandfather, too. The Warners have always buried people. I know it sounds like a creepy profession.

Not everyone could do it and stay cheerful and brave, but my father manages."

"Do you ever feel creepy in your house late at night?" Jamie had to know the most personal things about people she liked.

"No, but there's one thing about it I hate. *Hate*," she repeated for emphasis.

"What?"

"My friends will stop by for visits, but no one, not anyone, will ever sleep over at my house."

"Never?"

"Never," Zoe said. "I used to ask Kai or the twins. They'd look nervous and say, 'Oh, why don't you sleep over at my house instead?' Or they'd make up some excuse." There was real hurt in Zoe's voice and eyes. "I know it's because of the cadavers downstairs and the roomful of caskets. I can't believe I'm telling you all these crazy things."

Jamie had never met anyone like Zoe. All her life she'd wanted a friend who talked and listened the way Zoe did.

"Well, the cadavers are dead. They can't hurt anyone. I'm surprised because Kai and the twins seem so brave," Jamie said.

Zoe looked at her cautiously. There was an uncomfortable silence, and Jamie thought Zoe wasn't going to say anything.

"They *are* brave," Zoe finally said. "They take a lot of chances about some things, but death is different. Most people think anything to do with death is very creepy. They think the embalmer might be hanging out in the kitchen with one of his embalming syringes. What if they have to shake his hand? Worse, what if a body snatcher comes at midnight and takes *them* by mistake instead of the dead guy downstairs?"

"I'll sleep over at your house," Jamie blurted impulsively. "I'd love to. I like unusual places. Nothing scares me."

"Really?" Zoe asked.

"Oh, sure," Jamie said. "Listen, I live in Booger Hollow. We have a nice house, but it's Booger Hollow all the same. You know how people feel about that neighborhood."

Zoe smiled. The whole of her tiny, perfect face smiled. "Tomorrow is Friday. How about then?"

"Oh, sure," Jamie said again. "Friday's fine with me." The thought of being with Zoe at her house sent a shaft of yellow light through Jamie's mind, like a door opening.

Conversation flowered between them. They talked about Mr. Hughes-Walter and how St. Agnes Hall used to be a convent. Jamie lost her sense of time. It no longer mattered that they were sitting in front of the principal's office waiting to get bawled out. Finally the school bell rang and girls in green and white streamed out of the building. Miss Pickney still hadn't called them in.

When Zoe saw Kai walking toward them, she whispered, "Don't say anything to anyone about tomorrow night. Okay?"

"Sure," Jamie said, and shrugged, but she wondered why Zoe wouldn't want anyone to know.

Kai joined them and shucked her backpack. The twins followed her. They had soft brown hair that swung around their cheekbones. It was carelessly held in place on one side by a barrette. They always looked ready to laugh. At the start of school, Jamie had put them down in her mental notes as possibly dumb. Later, because of their answers to Mr. Hughes-Walter's questions in class, she realized they were just always ready for all-out fun.

The secretary walked out. "Miss Pickney can't break away. She read the note, though. You're both to write a two-page essay about the importance of staying on task, not wasting class time. Do you understand?"

"Staying on task," Zoe said.

"Not wasting class time," Jamie added. "Two pages."

The secretary nodded. "Turn it in to Mr. Hughes-Walter in the morning."

"Yes, ma'am," Zoe said. She gathered up her purse and backpack. "We're going to an after-school art class at the university. See you tomorrow, Jamie," Zoe said over her shoulder.

"Tomorrow." Jamie smiled. She shouldered her backpack and turned toward home.

"That new girl," Jamie heard Kai's whisper. "Isn't she awfully tall?"

"She's okay," Zoe answered.

Jamie drifted down the street to Booger Hollow. Her backpack slopped from side to side. She shriveled on her heels, shoulders hunched. She knew Kai meant for her words to be heard. This sent a wave of discomfort all through her, the way the ruff on the back of Tank's neck stood up when he heard a noise he didn't like.

Then Jamie thought of the afternoon with Zoe and Friday night to come. Zoe didn't want her friends to know

Jamie was spending the night. Is it me, Jamie wondered, or would she try to keep a visit from anyone a secret?

She thought about her old private-citizen plan—keeping to herself, making perfect grades. What she really wanted was to be Zoe's friend, to fit in and belong.

When Jamie came in from school, Gus was watching their mother mix batter for a wedding cake. If you cut Mother, Jamie thought, flour would probably ooze out.

"Her eyebrows don't even match," Gus said abruptly.

"What does that have to do with anything?" Their mother pushed her hair back from her forehead with the back of her hand.

"Well, she's not perfect either," Gus said.

"What's going on?" Jamie asked. "Whose eyebrows don't match?"

"His teacher's." Mrs. McClure frowned at Gus. "Seems Gus was afraid something was wrong with his eyes, so he stood behind the kids with glasses and memorized what they said on the eye chart."

"He *cheated* on a vision test?" Jamie asked, chortling.

"I'm glad you think it's funny that your little brother could have been flattened in traffic," her mother said above the whir of the big mixer.

Jamie looked at Gus. He had taken his shirt off and his ribs were sharp and white. She tried to imagine his little face with glasses.

"Anyway," their mother said, "you two get on out of here and let me bake my cake. You can have some leftover canapés from the party last night, but no television."

Jamie was reluctant to leave the cool kitchen that smelled of vanilla and sugar. She took a notebook and pen from her backpack and balanced the plate of canapés. She motioned to Gus and he followed her out to the backyard. They sat on the ground under a huge oak tree, the plate between them.

"What's a canopy?" Gus asked.

"*Canapé*, Gus," Jamie corrected. "It's a French word for couch."

"Doesn't look like a couch to me," Gus said. He held a meat-stuffed grape leaf just beyond the tip of his nose. He closed one eye and looked at it with the other.

"It's sort of a little seat for whatever you decide to put on top," Jamie said.

They especially liked the hors d'oeuvres with the silly names: pigs in a blanket, seafood pretties, angels on horseback, and henhouse nomads.

Jamie ate a few hot quackers, which were really just barbecued chicken wings. Before Mrs. McClure began working so hard, she'd tried out all her recipes on Jamie and her father. Gus was eating baby food back then. Thinking about it made her sad.

Jamie moved to the tree swing and opened her notebook to write the essay for Miss Pickney. Gus shinnied up the oak tree. There was a private shady cave inside the branches that used to be hers, but she'd given it to Gus last summer.

Tank came across the yard and ate the rest of the canapés, saliva slathering his teeth. He flung himself with a contented sigh beneath the tree. Almost instantly he was asleep, wheezing and groaning.

The tree swing creaked, setting up a rhythm. Jamie was on the first paragraph when Mr. Graves poked his ruddy face through the privet hedge that separated his yard from theirs. Jamie started. His blue eyes were as bright as the eyes of a wild thing, peering through the hedge.

"Jamie," Gus whispered loudly from above. He monkeyed over to a branch away from the hedge.

"Hello, Mr. Graves," Jamie said. "How is your sister?"

"She went back to San Antonio. Um. I'm afraid I've got some unhappy news to report," he said. "I think you'd better come to my yard."

Jamie motioned to Gus and reluctantly pushed through the hedge. Gus followed her.

She'd kept an eye on Mr. Graves for further signs of craziness since spying on him. He did his jumping jacks and push-ups on the patio in the mornings. Late each afternoon he sat alone at the peacock-blue table in the yard and watched his bees flying from the hives to the creek and the alfalfa field, and back again.

Today he wore a safari vest slung over his T-shirt, making him look more like a jungle explorer than a beekeeper. Still, he seemed smaller, diminished by Pearlie's absence, and there were dark pouches under his eyes.

"I was taking a nap this afternoon when I heard a screeching followed by a moaning that nearly took the hair off my head." Mr. Graves rubbed his beard.

"What was it?" Gus asked anxiously. "Did it smell bad? Could it have been a Sasquatch?"

Mr. Graves looked at Gus. "No. There's no such thing as Sasquatches. It was my cat, dead now, and in a condition to take the sight out of a good eye."

Jamie looked around the yard. The sun burned gold

through the trees, and rainbows shimmered in the spray from a sprinkler. The same orange cat she'd seen the night she visited was draped limp and noodlelike on one of the blue chairs at the table.

"There's your cat, Mr. Graves," she said, and pointed.

"Oh, that's Big Orange," Mr. Graves said. "The dead cat was Skunk. He was black and white. I buried him there, under the tree."

Under a pecan tree close to the privet hedge was a small, freshly dug mound of earth.

"That's just really horrible," Jamie said, meaning it. How many tragedies would Mr. Graves have to endure? Not that you could compare the two.

"Yes," he said. "The poor old furball hadn't even used up all nine lives yet."

They stood in an awkward silence while a squirrel chattered at them through the leaves of the pecan tree. Jamie had an uneasy feeling. Why was he telling them this?

As though he'd read her mind, Mr. Graves clucked his tongue against the roof of his mouth. "I believe your big dog killed Skunk."

"What?" Jamie said.

"When I ran out, I think it was your dog that high-tailed it back through the privet hedge."

"I don't believe it!" Jamie said. "Tank's never—I mean a few frogs, maybe—but he's never hurt a cat."

"Yeah," Gus said. "Tank looks mean, but he's even afraid of the vacuum cleaner."

At the mention of his name Tank came shambling through the hedge.

"Tank's got something in his mouth!" yelled Gus.

A black leg and a long hairless tail hung out of the big dog's mouth. The tail curled up over Tank's mouth, giving the appearance of a mustache. Gus turned a pale green.

"Is that a rat in his mouth?" Jamie screamed.

"I'm afraid so," Mr. Graves said. "It probably came from the fields across the road."

Jamie looked at Mr. Graves, but he just slowly raised his eyebrows and spread his hands as if to say "I told you so."

"Bad dog!" Jamie yelled. "Go home now!"

Tank grunted, still struggling with the rat, and pushed slowly back through the hedge.

Really, there was just no end to what could happen. Tank ate rats *and* he was a cat killer? Jamie didn't believe it. She'd never known him to even *chase* a cat.

"Tank is my little brother." Gus's chin quivered.

"How's that?" Mr. Graves asked.

"I begged for a baby brother," Gus said mournfully. "They gave me Tank instead."

"Ah." Mr. Graves pushed out his lower lip thoughtfully.

"My mother doesn't like Tank." Gus stood with his shoulders hunched, his eyes like those of a threatened bird.

"Could I speak to you in private, Mr. Graves?" Jamie said, watching Gus.

"Certainly."

They walked to the patio, which was sheltered like a tree house by a large fig tree. A dozen goldfish scattered to the lily pads when they passed a fountain. There were so many things to look at in Mr. Graves's yard. Backyards are always more interesting than front yards, Jamie thought.

"My brother is having some trouble at school," Jamie started. "And my mother has all these parties to cater this fall. She's really edgy, you see."

"Yes."

"And as it is, Tank has to stay outside because of her business. The health department doesn't like animals where people cook. What I'm getting to is this: If you tell her about Tank and your cat, I'm afraid she'll give him away."

"Are you suggesting that I *shouldn't* tell your mother about this?" Mr. Graves asked.

She looked at Gus. Glasses would probably mean more teasing at school. Jamie's heart beat faster. "Losing Tank would be very bad for Gus. Gus talks to Tank a lot. I think he even believes Tank protects him." How to explain about hyenas and Sasquatches? She wouldn't even try. She didn't really think Tank had killed this Skunk cat, but she was still so ashamed of her behavior at Pearlie's funeral that she wasn't about to argue.

"So I was thinking," Jamie continued, "we could never make up for your cat, but maybe we could do something for you."

There was a queasy silence. Mr. Graves was hard to read.

"That fountain with the goldfish, for example," Jamie said. "We could clean it out. No offense, but it's a little smelly."

Mr. Graves swatted away a whining mosquito. "I

don't know," he said. "I feel a little bad about keeping an important piece of news from your mother."

Jamie looked out to the bee yard, which could be clearly seen from the porch. "Well, maybe I could help you with the beehives," Jamie quickly offered. "Pearlie told me you still had comb honey to put up in jars before you get the hives ready for fall."

At this he raised his eyebrows so they looked like little V-shaped temples on his forehead.

"Bees can be very frightening for beginners," Mr. Graves said.

"I'm not afraid of bees or anything else. I could wear that white suit and veil Pearlie wore when she helped you, and her gloves," Jamie said, and immediately wished she'd kept her mouth shut. He might not want just anyone wearing Pearlie's clothes so soon.

"Well, that's a thought," he said to her surprise.

"Gus could clean out the fountain while we're in the bee yard. He enjoys stuff like that, and it's too shallow to be dangerous."

"Come over on Saturday and we'll try it," he said.

"Okay," Jamie said, and offered him a smile as a peace token. She felt relieved as she walked away.

Once she and Gus were back in their own yard, Jamie pushed herself in the tree swing.

"What did he say?" Gus asked. Tank jumped up on Gus's thighs, his head bobbing. The rat was nowhere in sight. Gus scratched behind the dog's ears and gave him pats on his side that made deep, hollow sounds.

"He said he won't tell Mom about Tank if we help him. Would you be willing to clean out that fountain with the goldfish on Saturday?"

Gus shrugged. "Sure. He's got a lot of neat stuff over there. But I don't think Tank killed his old cat."

"I don't either," Jamie said. What did Mr. Graves really want? she wondered.

Chapter

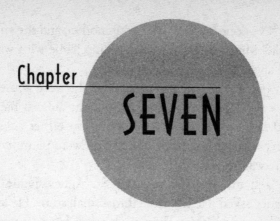

SEVEN

On Friday evening Jamie walked to Zoe's house through the lavender twilight, her overnight bag in her hand. Her mother's pleased expression was still in her mind.

"You've been invited to the Warners'?" she'd asked, a surprised look on her face. "I knew St. Agnes would be good for you."

Jamie wore shorts and her favorite yellow blouse, and she'd packed her best cotton nightgown.

Her father had sent a charm bracelet for her last birthday. It was a string of hearts. She was certain his new wife had picked it out, but she liked it anyway. Jamie put it on for luck just before she left.

Zoe's house was massive. A huge stone chimney guarded one end of the roof, and clusters of tiny-paned windows huddled in groups under the eaves. A sign over the heavy oak door read WARNER'S FUNERAL HOME, SINCE 1902.

She had just rung the doorbell when Mr. Warner answered. "Well, come on in," he said, looking amused and pleased. They stood smiling in the entrance hall.

"I've done business with your mother, and she's a great cook," Mr. Warner said, surrounding Jamie with warmth and approval.

Mrs. Warner came in with Zoe. She wore glasses and her eyes were pale green. Her straight auburn hair was held away from her face by combs on either side. She didn't wear makeup and her clothes were plain, but her smile was kind and friendly.

"Tell me, how do you like St. Agnes, Jamie?" Mr. Warner asked. He led them into a small study. He looked as if he could be Mrs. Warner's brother. His eyes were the same green. And his gentle manner was just like Zoe's. The concerned expression he held while he listened to Jamie's impressions of sixth grade was Zoe's, too.

"We're so pleased you're spending the night, Jamie." Mrs. Warner's smile was big.

Jamie followed Zoe into the kitchen, where she fished a couple of Cokes out of the refrigerator.

"Let's go up to my room," Zoe said. She moved up the wide staircase as quick and light as a butterfly. The prospect of company in the big gloomy house seemed to make her more animated than usual.

Zoe's room had high ceilings and a four-poster bed with ruffled snow-white pillow shams. A cool breeze fluttered the starched curtains at the window. Shelves encircling the entire room held all of Zoe's books and stuffed animals.

"I can't get rid of anything." Zoe shook her head. "I've had a lot of these things since I was born."

"I love your room," Jamie said as she walked around inspecting things. "Did you paint these?" she asked, looking at tiny pictures of animals and flowers on small easels. On the desk were a jar of water, several brushes, and scattered sheets of paper with sketches and paintings of panda bears.

"Yes," Zoe said. "I take art lessons from Dr. Weston at the university."

"They're really good," Jamie said.

Zoe laughed softly. "Sometimes I make believe I'm in art school in Paris. Last night I was at an outdoor café with my friends Dominique and François. We were speaking French and drinking coffee."

"I do stuff like that, too," said Jamie, whose own favorite fantasy was talking to her imaginary big sister.

"Well"—Zoe colored—"last night I got carried away, and my father stuck his head in and said, 'Who are you talking to?'"

"What did you say?"

"I told him I was practicing my book report."

"That was quick thinking," Jamie said. "Every now and then when I talk to my imaginary older sister in the mirror my little brother hears me. He's so scared of everything that he thinks I'm seeing ghosts or something. I don't ever get to be alone."

"I wish I had a little brother," Zoe said.

"He's cute, but my mother's so busy that she pushes him off on me all the time. I feel bad, but I'm really getting tired of it. He follows me everywhere."

"It sounds pretty good to me," Zoe said. "When you're an only child, sometimes you get *too* much attention from your parents. I think it would be fun to have a little brother around to talk to."

"You wouldn't have much privacy. Gus is afraid of the dark, so he sleeps in my room most of the time," Jamie said.

"Well," Zoe said, "maybe that would get old, but I've always wanted someone younger than me in the family. I think about it a lot at Christmas for some reason."

Jamie liked hanging around Zoe's room, just talking. She thought Zoe was the easiest person to talk to she'd ever known.

Zoe's room was as cheerful and bright as the rest of the house was somber. Her mother obviously wanted to make up for the gloomy life below. Jamie's eye caught a framed photograph on Zoe's bookcase. She took it down and looked at it closely while Zoe described how dull it was to decorate the Christmas tree with no one but her parents.

The picture was of Zoe and Kai and one of the twins; Jamie couldn't be sure which one. They looked about five, younger than Gus, and they wore dresses and sat on a bench. Zoe was in the middle. She looked downward, a big smile on her face, the tips of her shoes touching the ground. Kai, her hair impossibly short even then, was whispering something to Zoe, her hand cupped protectively around Zoe's ear. Merit or Vivica, whichever one it was, sat up straight, one hand on Zoe's shoulder, the other in her lap.

Jamie's spirits plunged. What was I thinking? she wondered. These girls had been friends as far back as their memory went. There would be no room for her in Zoe's world.

The doorbell rang, and Jamie put the photograph back on the shelf. There was a friendly commotion downstairs, and she looked over at Zoe, who was wide-eyed and obviously perplexed.

Zoe murmured, "They never come by on Friday."

There were muffled footsteps and Kai's hoarse voice on the stairway. "You have to hear this, Zoe," Kai called. "Merit and Vivica are having a real laugh riot over this."

"After school, Elmer spit this huge glob of tobacco that looked like puke on the rosebushes in the courtyard, so Kai says, 'Give me some of that, Elmer. I want some.' So he handed her this really ugly brown thing and she bit off a piece and *chewed* it!" Merit stumbled laughing into the room.

"No lie, Zoe." Vivica was behind her. "So then Kai spit some into the rosebush while he was watching, and then he blew his nose into his hands, and she did, too."

Merit stopped, startled, when she saw Jamie. "Hi," she said.

"Hi." Jamie lifted her hand in an awkward wave. Why were Kai and the twins here?

"Um, we were just talking about Elmer," Vivica said, "that really disgusting custodian at school."

The twins couldn't have looked more surprised to see her than if she were one of Gus's hyenas, thought Jamie, and Zoe looked as though she wished she were anywhere else in the world.

Kai raised an eyebrow at Jamie, then turned to Zoe. "We need to talk about some stuff, so we're going to the twins' house."

"I don't think I can go," Zoe said timidly.

"Why not?" Kai demanded. "It's the weekend, and I brought this bag of polish to paint our toenails."

"Why don't we just stay here?" Zoe said.

"I *said* we need to discuss some things," Kai said, trying to signal Zoe with her eyes. "Maybe Jamie could stop by some other time."

This is not happening, Jamie thought. I am not in this room being flattened like a fly. Jamie wondered why Zoe didn't just tell them she was invited over. The doorbell rang again, twice.

"I'll get the door," Zoe said, and escaped from the room.

Jamie clenched her fingers into the palms of her hands. Out of nowhere she found her voice. "I didn't stop by. I was invited to spend the night."

"Here?" Merit asked. "At Zoe's?"

"Yes."

"We don't spend the night at Zoe's," Kai said. "No one has ever spent the night here."

"I am," Jamie said quietly. "I'm spending the night here."

"I'll bet that's the pizza man downstairs," Vivica said. "He always rings twice. Let's stay here and eat with Zoe and Jamie. We can always go to our house later, Kai."

Kai shrugged in a disinterested way, but the what's-going-on-here? look on her face gave her away. Amazing, Jamie thought. She's jealous because I'm here, and Zoe doesn't want to get Kai stirred up.

Zoe came in with a large pizza box. Her mother followed with napkins and Cokes. "We have more than enough for everyone," Mrs. Warner said.

"You're all invited to stay," Zoe added. "We always order too much because my dad and I like cold pizza for breakfast."

72

There was an uncomfortable silence while they ate, but after they finished, no one made a move to leave.

Kai abruptly went to the bathroom. When she came back, she was wheezing a little. She pitched a bag to Zoe. "Here's the fingernail polish."

Zoe unzipped it. "Great!" she said, forcing cheerfulness. She looked at Jamie. "See, Kai has two older sisters in college. They have all this makeup and stuff that they get tired of and leave behind when they go back to school."

Zoe poured the contents of the bag onto the floor. There were bottles of green, pink, lavender, blue, and gold nail polish.

Kai took a small plastic bag out of her shirt pocket. "I've got some rhinestones and little tattoos you can put on your nails while they're drying, too."

"I know what," Zoe said. "Let's paint our toenails all different colors."

"Fingernails, too," Jamie said, and immediately regretted it. She'd bitten her fingernails to nothing since school started. There wouldn't be much to paint.

Kai leveled her unsettling eyes on Jamie. "What were you—hatched yesterday? We can't have painted fingernails at St. Agnes," she said. "But toenails can't be seen."

A fist of anxiety tightened in Jamie's stomach.

They sat on the floor in a circle, the bottles of nail polish spread out in the middle. A floor lamp cast a pool of warm yellow light. The twins lowered their sooty lashes over dark gray eyes as they carefully painted each toe a different color.

Kai shook a bottle of green polish. She looked at Zoe. "My sisters called, and they're coming home the first

73

weekend in October. They promised to take you and the twins and me shopping in San Antonio."

"Really?" Zoe asked quietly.

"Yeah," Kai said, "and we might get to spend the night there if your mother will let you."

"My parents are overprotective," Zoe explained to Jamie.

"I know what you mean," Jamie lied. Mrs. McClure didn't have time to be overprotective.

"You should try to get on their nerves more, Zoe," Vivica suggested.

"Yeah," Kai said. "Act out some symptoms of those mental-hospital patients. They'd be ready to let you go anywhere."

Zoe looked at Jamie and smiled a little. "Vivica and Merit's mom is a child psychiatrist, and she has all these huge books in her office at home. The worst one is named *The State Mental Hospital*. It tells terrible stories about real people. We used to play a game where one of us was the patient and made up a problem, and the others were the psychiatrists and they had to figure it out and cure it and if they couldn't, then—"

"Don't tell an outsider all that stuff!" Kai said. She put a star rhinestone on a pink toenail and smeared it.

The twins looked up at Kai's angry face. In an injured tone Zoe said, "It was just a game we played in the fourth grade, Kai. Why are you acting like this?"

Jamie's throat felt tight. She wanted to run home and take Gus on a flashlight walk or help her mother decorate one of her wedding cakes with flowers and leaves made of colored icing.

"Well," Kai said, "we've already got Abigail Frank breathing down our throats, probably even following us, and Jamie overheard all that stuff Abigail said in the bathroom."

"I'm not going to tell anyone," Jamie said.

"How do we know that?" Kai asked. "You could have a big mouth—*huge*, even."

"Well," Jamie said, "I don't have a big mouth. Who would I tell anyway? I don't know anyone that well, and I don't even know what that circle thing you were talking about is."

Another uneasy silence filled the room while the girls finished painting their toenails.

"Ta-da!" Kai finally said, and stretched her feet out for all to see. "Rainbow toes!"

"Pretty," Jamie said, and nodded—goofily, she thought—like a marionette.

A light rain began to fall, and the low throbbing of crickets came through the open window. Mrs. Warner came in to tell Merit and Vivica and Kai that the twins' father would pick them up in forty-five minutes.

"So," Kai said when she left, putting the bottles of polish back into the bag. "Zoe says you live in Booger Hollow. What's that like?" she casually asked, and reached for a crust of pizza.

Jamie shrugged and looked down at her multicolored toes.

She wanted to tell them that it wasn't what most people thought—a spooky neighborhood where old people lived. But she also wanted to tell them that, in a way, all of that was true and that the stories and legends the neighbors told were part of what made it special to her.

The others might be interested, but she was afraid of Kai, of her superior little smile and the way she didn't feel she had to be friendly or even polite.

A sense of expectancy hung in the air. On impulse Jamie said, "It's great! I know the weirdest stories."

Merit's eyebrows shot upward. "Things that really happened in Booger Hollow?"

"Well, according to my next-door neighbor," Jamie said.

"Pearlie Wu?" With a quick motion of her hands, Zoe did her hair up in a knot on top of her head.

Jamie nodded. "She told me lots of stories that were supposed to have really happened in Booger Hollow. She lived there a long time."

Her heart did cartwheels. Finally, something she was good at—storytelling!

"Oh, good," Zoe said, as if determined to lighten the mood in the room. She got up and carefully placed Merit's red Windbreaker over the lamp, throwing Jamie's shadow across the room, large and looming.

Zoe's mood change was infectious. Vivica and Merit's gray eyes sparkled like smoked glass, their faces ghoulish in the eerie red light.

"Please, none of those escaped-from-an-insane-asylum stories," Kai said in a bored voice.

"I thought you loved ghost stories, Kai," Vivica said.

Jamie ignored Kai. "Well, this is the last one Pearlie told me," she began. "Years ago, before any of us were born, these cousins got married for mad love. Their parents were against it and wouldn't come to the wedding or give them any money for a honeymoon. They bought the house two doors down from where we live today. It was falling apart, but it was all they could afford.

"They spent their first night there. Unfortunately, it was a night just like tonight—no moon. When they turned the lights out, they heard noises—strange hissing and slithering noises."

Jamie paused to draw a calculated breath. Her eyes circled the group, roping in the twins and Zoe in particular. Zoe leaned forward, her mouth open and her hands gripping her knees. Kai watched Jamie without batting her eyes.

Jamie lowered her voice to a hoarse whisper. "When the husband went to check on the noise, his foot went through the rotten wood of the floorboards, and he stepped into a nest of snakes."

"Snakes?" Vivica asked.

"Rattlesnakes," Jamie said. "There were, well, I don't know how many rattlesnakes, but a lot. They struck the husband again and again as he moved. He screamed out, 'Don't move, my darling! Just stay safely in bed. Whatever you do, don't move an inch!' And for hours she did what he said. Can you imagine hearing those snakes rattle their tails, his screams, and knowing he was being struck again and again?

"All the while," Jamie continued, "the wife couldn't move one inch because for all she knew, there could have been a coiled rattlesnake on the bed ready to strike her at any movement."

They were glommed on to her every word now, even

Kai. Jamie leaned closer, dropping her voice lower. "There was the poor husband. There were too many rattlesnake bites to count, his *whole* body a mass of bites. At first light, the rattlesnakes went down to their nests under the floorboards like they had never been there at all. No one really saw them come, and no one saw them leave."

"Did that really happen?" Kai demanded. "Tell me the truth."

"It happened, all right," Jamie said, glancing down at her painted toenails. "The people who live there now completely redid the house. But they say that sometimes, late at night, they hear hissing sounds like a thousand coiled snakes, and sobbing outside."

"Why sobbing?" Kai asked.

"The wife left town after her husband's funeral. She lived to be a very old woman with white hair. Of course, she spent the rest of her life reliving the snake-night honeymoon again and again in her mind, until she went insane and had to be tied to her bed. She's dead now, but sometimes she comes back and cries for her lost love."

Kai wrapped her arms around her knees. Her gaze on Jamie was steady, intense. "Tell us another one."

Jamie felt good, somehow, to be passing on some of Pearlie Wu's stories. Even if they were "bunkum," as her mother said, they were a part of Pearlie and Booger Hollow.

"This happened farther down the street just a few years ago," Jamie said. "Every night at bedtime this family was surprised by a masked man at the window. He had bushy, greasy hair, and he wore a purple fluorescent mask

78

that covered his face. It glowed in the dark as he went from window to window."

Jamie's voice became hushed, confidential, as she described how he never left footprints or trampled the flower beds. She spread her hands, and shadows jumped onto the wall.

"He just seemed to float from window to window. Finally the father had had enough. He was a construction worker, and one night he shot the mask with one of those high-pressure nail guns. It pinned the mask to a tree, and nothing was left but a hideous raw head and bloody, dripping bones. When the police came, there was no head, no blood, no body. Only the mask. So the police put the mask in a bag for evidence, but it disintegrated."

"Did he ever come back?" Kai asked.

"Every now and then people on our street complain of seeing the masked stranger." Jamie hesitated and looked at the ceiling for a moment. "I've never told anyone this, but one night last summer I saw it," she lied.

"No way," said Merit.

"Oh, yes," Jamie said in a firm voice. She darted an uneasy glance out the window for effect. "I was alone in the kitchen, and it floated in front of our window. Its face glowed purple, and it smiled at me. Every hair on my head moved.

"I used to say I'd like to see a ghost," Jamie continued dramatically, "or have some kind of psychic experience. But now I know I was wrong. I think it can drive people insane and make their hair white."

As luck would have it, an ambulance wail cut through the night like a comet. It was then that the neighborhood dogs began to howl. Faintly at first, a yelp here and there, but within minutes every dog in the area howled into the night. Perfect, thought Jamie.

Kai watched Jamie with grudging admiration, and the twins' eyes were wide and shining. Zoe's face glowed. After all, Jamie's coming to the ancient house had made Zoe's friends stay over, if only for dinner, and out of curiosity or jealousy. Sitting on the floor of Zoe's room in the eerie red light, Jamie felt buoyant. She might not be an old friend, but if she played her cards right, maybe it wouldn't matter.

Chapter

EIGHT

After Kai and the twins left, Zoe and Jamie said good night to the Warners, who closed their bedroom door.

"I'm starving," Zoe said.

They went downstairs to the kitchen in their night-gowns. Zoe pulled a big bowl of grapes and cherries from the refrigerator.

Jamie pitched grapes into the air, catching them in her mouth, while Zoe spit cherry pits across the kitchen into the trash can.

"So you like scary things, huh?" Zoe asked.

"Yeah, I don't think I'd love living in Booger Hollow if I didn't," Jamie said.

"Do you want to see the embalming room?" Zoe asked.

"The embalming room," Jamie repeated, dazed, as though it were what she had always wanted to see. She blinked and swallowed hard.

Before she had time to think, Zoe grabbed her arm and pulled her through the kitchen and down a long, dimly lit hallway. When they turned the corner, Jamie saw a flight of stairs going down to a door with a neon sign above it that said ABSOLUTELY NO ADMITTANCE. AUTHORIZED PERSONNEL ONLY.

Zoe started down the stairs as if a playroom were at the bottom. Jamie said, "Wait. Are we *allowed* in that room?"

"I am. You're not." Zoe said, and shrugged. "But stick with me. I can get you into all the best places."

Jamie giggled at this, causing Zoe to laugh.

"Are there any authorized personnel down there?" called Zoe softly between giggles.

Jamie felt frightened and giddy at the same time, as though her nerves were unraveling again as they had done at Pearlie's funeral. At least this time she didn't have to feel bad about laughing.

"Come on." Zoe pulled her arm again.

"Wait," Jamie said again. "Is a dead person down there?"

"The deceased," Zoe corrected. "We call them the *deceased*."

Jamie followed Zoe down the creaking stairs. When Zoe opened the door, she grabbed Jamie's hand. A dense, powerful odor filled the air.

"What *is* that?" Jamie whispered, tiptoeing into the room after Zoe.

"Formaldehyde and pancake makeup," Zoe whispered back. "You can't make it go away, even when a body isn't in here."

A quick glance left Jamie relieved that no dead body lay on the wide slab across the room. The walls were of mottled concrete that looked like headstones on the graves in cemeteries. Jamie felt a bad case of the shivers coming on. She stood in front of a glass-fronted chest full of bottles, tubes, and boxes.

"What is all this stuff?" Jamie asked, still whispering.

"Chemicals, makeup, things like that," Zoe said. "Why are we whispering, anyway?"

This set Jamie off on another fit of nervous giggles bordering on hysteria.

"Do you really come in when the…bodies…are here?" Jamie asked.

"Sometimes when Wilma, the beautician, is working," Zoe said. "I talk to her while she puts the makeup on. She's the funniest person I've ever known."

Jamie was shocked. What could be funny in a room like this? She thought of Pearlie Wu, who had never liked makeup. It must have been this Wilma person's idea to make Pearlie's cheeks pink and her mouth bright red.

The old bones of the house suddenly creaked, sending Jamie and Zoe scurrying back upstairs.

Once they were settled in Zoe's bed, Jamie asked, "Did Wilma think Pearlie was funny when she was dead?"

"Oh, no, Jamie," said Zoe. "I'm sorry. I should have explained. My father teaches everyone to have respect for the deceased. Wilma doesn't ever laugh about the dead *person*, just about death itself. It's easier to live with death if you laugh about it. Otherwise you'd be scared a lot of the time."

"My mother calls cheerful people happy campers. That's what she'd call you. She'd think you were really grown up for your age, too."

"I've always lived above dead people," Zoe said, clicking off the bedside lamp. She pulled the starched white covers up. "They don't scare me. There are some live people that do, though."

"No kidding," Jamie said, thinking of how she liked ghost stories but felt uneasy around Kai and Mr. Graves.

"You're the only person I've ever taken to the embalming room," Zoe said sleepily.

"Really?" Jamie asked. It was an odd honor, but she felt a pinch of pride.

"Really," Zoe said.

"I've never taken a friend in my mom's catering van with the wedding cake whirling around. You'd probably *hate* it, though. It would embarrass you completely."

"No, it wouldn't," Zoe said. "When I was little and saw that truck with the cake spinning around, I'd get so excited."

Zoe fell asleep like Gus: suddenly, leaving Jamie's mind jumping from Kai and the twins' unexpected visit, to her new friendship with Zoe, and the embalming room.

She had been struggling since Pearlie's funeral—her mind glazing over, really—with her own laughter in the face of death. Had Zoe just explained it? Her sleep came in fits and starts until she finally made herself think of Shangri-la and the crystal palace surrounded by face-painted guards.

As she walked home from Zoe's house the next morning, Jamie's thoughts were divided between her experiences the previous night and her promise to help Mr. Graves in the bee yard later.

"Well," her mother was saying to Gus when Jamie came in, "they're just television monsters, make-believe, nothing at all for a big boy like you to worry about."

Gus was at the kitchen table, sitting cross-legged on the chair, the table up to his neck. He held his fork with a small fist and stared at his egg. A little crust of milk ringed his mouth.

"What's going on?" Jamie asked, and dropped her bag on the floor.

"Oh, Gus watched the Midnight Creature Feature on television last night while I was cooking, and he didn't get much sleep." Her mother wore a full-front apron over her pants, and she looked prepared for anything. "I didn't sleep much either," she added, stretching her arms and arching her stiff back.

Suddenly her mother's face was full of hopeful questions. "Did you have fun at the Warners'?"

"Sure, I had a lot of fun," Jamie said. "But why did you let Gus watch something scary like that? That's how he heard about Sasquatches." Really, all she had to do was go away for one night and things fell apart. Sometimes her mother acted like an irresponsible kid where Gus was concerned. Gus was even wearing his pajamas wrong-side out.

"I didn't know," Jamie's mother said, and kissed Gus on the top of his head. "I thought he was watching cartoons."

"Children are supposed to be in *bed* late at night, Mother!" Jamie snapped.

"Know what they showed?" Gus asked. "These huge spiders that are hairy. They can jump four feet. If those suckers get you, you go crazy because they have a special kind of poison. And you weren't here, and I didn't have anyone to be with." He scowled at Jamie.

"Jamie's growing up, Gus," Mrs. McClure said. "She's making friends at St. Agnes, the kind of friends she'll know all her life. She can't be here all the time."

"He's just a little kid, Mother," Jamie persisted. "Let him make cookies or something when you're in the kitchen."

"Oh, calm down, Jamie," was all her mother said.

Gus sat huddled like an old man, rolling shreds of his toast into pellets.

Sometimes Jamie hated all the cooking that went on in their house. She woke up to the smells of cooking and fell asleep to the smells of cooking. Any time of the day she walked in and smelled cooking.

It occurred to Jamie that her mother treated food very gently. When Jamie helped her transport tall wedding cakes and plates of appetizers and pies with meringue toppings in the van, her mother would say again and again, "Now, let's be very careful with this," or "Turn on the air conditioner. Don't let that meringue get heated and sweat."

Jamie thought it wouldn't be a bad idea to write something across Gus's forehead. Some attention-getting word: "FRAGILE!" or "CAREFUL."

Was Gus any less important than food?

"Um, Mother, Gus and I are going to help Mr. Graves in his yard today," Jamie said.

Mrs. McClure was rolling out pastry. "I thought you said he was mean."

"We feel sorry for him," Jamie lied. "Hurry up and put that egg out of its misery, Gus. Finish up."

Gus's eyes lit up, and he started eating. Jamie ate finger sandwiches from a tray. They were filled with cream cheese and sliced cucumbers.

"Well, I think it's nice of you to spend time with Mr. Graves," Mrs. McClure said. "He's all alone and needs his neighbors."

"He's got a cat," Gus said. "He had two, but…" Gus slapped a hand over his mouth.

Jamie shot Gus a warning look, but her mother was absorbed in fluting pie shells.

When they pushed through the hedge, Mr. Graves sat under the old fig tree at the peacock-blue table on his patio. He was hunched over an open notebook.

"Hi," Gus called.

Mr. Graves looked up at them, his eyes a somber blue. He got up and walked toward them. Jamie had the distinct feeling he was glad to see them.

"I caught all the goldfish from the fountain and put them in that big washtub over there," Mr. Graves said, looking at Gus. "All you have to do is take out the dead lily pads and bail out the dirty water with that coffee can. Then we'll wash the fountain out and put clean water in."

Jamie and Gus looked in the washtub. Mr. Graves handed Gus a box of goldfish food. When he sprinkled it over the surface, a bubble came to the top, paused, and broke. Several black and orange goldfish arched upward to gobble the food and dived again, swimming in a pattern of arrowheads. They seemed to vanish and reappear like lights going on and off.

"They look like tigers, all black and gold," Jamie said.

"Halloween fish." Gus's eyes were big and bright. He reached for one and it swam away.

"Pearlie brought these fish home years ago," Mr. Graves said. "They've been around a long time."

"Jamie says I'm a good worker," Gus told Mr. Graves.

"We'll soon find out, then, won't we?" Mr. Graves said.

They left Gus to his chores, and Jamie followed Mr. Graves down the garden path to the honey house. It was just a small one-room rock house that was fashioned after the cottage Mr. Graves lived in.

Jamie didn't know what to expect, but when Mr. Graves opened the door, the sweet odor of honey permeated the air. The same five-gallon containers with spigots that she and Pearlie had used to pour honey into jars lined the walls. A large freezer took up space on one wall. Metal extractors and hive tools lay on a worktable. A golden slosh of honey was in the bottom of a honey ripener. The floor was sticky, and it was warm inside.

"Pearlie described all of this to me, but I never really knew what the honey house looked like inside," Jamie said.

Pearlie's white coveralls and bee veil hung from a hook on the wall. Her gloves lay on the bench, still molded to the shape of her hands. Stunned, Jamie stood there and felt her own hands grow cold.

"Just slip those coveralls over your clothes, and I'll help you with the veil," Mr. Graves said. When Jamie didn't move, Mr. Graves said, "Go on. Pearlie wouldn't mind."

The coveralls, which were a bit short on her, tied above her ankles, and Mr. Graves put a helmet with a mesh veil attached onto her head. Jamie slipped Pearlie's gloves on while Mr. Graves gathered his equipment. She felt like an astronaut.

They left the honey house, Mr. Graves carrying a little hand-held smoker. It was stuffed with burning burlap and had a bellows on the side. He had a hive tool in one pocket and a bee brush in his other hand. He didn't wear any special clothing.

It was a short hike from the honey house to the shady grove of pecan trees that was the bee yard. The hives stood in the soft dirt in neat rows. Jamie heard the bees hum, and it seemed as if the air was full of wings and buzzing and sweet smells.

Each hive was made up of several stacked-up wooden boxes that could be lifted off one another. Mr. Graves went to the last row of hives. Bees flitting all about him, he puffed a few plumes of smoke from the smoker into the entrance of the first hive in the row. He spoke to Jamie for the first time since they'd left the honey house.

"Smoke calms the bees. They dive their heads into honey cells and start eating. I don't know why. No one does. Maybe the fumes make them think a forest fire is coming and they better load up before they escape."

A few bees zinged at Jamie, buzzing and stalling before her veil, making her jump back. Jamie felt prickles and itches all over just seeing that many bees. Her breath came faster, and she wanted to turn and run back home. Why would anyone want to do this?

When Mr. Graves lifted the outer cover off the hive, the bees danced around as though at the end of long elastic bands. He blew more smoke down inside and lifted off the inner cover. It was crusted with crawling bees. Jamie became aware that she was in a bone-stiff trance, intolerably tense.

"Are you okay?" he asked.

She nodded. "I think so."

"Well, just remember: If you don't bother them, they won't bother you. Also, you're protected by that suit."

She took a couple of deep breaths and clenched her trembling hands.

Bees crawled across Mr. Graves's neck and down his arms and hands. Jamie watched in eerie fascination as a few crawled in his beard.

"Don't they sting you?" she asked.

"It doesn't hurt much. Your body actually gets used to the venom."

He tranquilly blew more plumes of smoke from the smoker. He used his hive tool to lift out several rectangular frames, then brushed the bees off the frames, which were capped with beeswax.

"I'm going to be handing frames like this one to you. I don't know if you noticed the freezer in the honey house, but you can't miss it. Just stack these inside and come back for more."

Jamie was glad to have a task so that she could move around. Mr. Graves continued down the rows, puffing smoke, taking frames out, and brushing the bees away.

She felt herself relax a little as she moved back and forth between the honey house and the bee yard.

She noticed for the first time the small piece of black cloth tied to each of the thirty beehives. It was the same cloth she'd seen Mr. Graves tie when he told the bees of Pearlie's death. Jamie vowed to find a way to ask about this.

After Mr. Graves handed her the frames from the last hive, they went back to the honey house together. The sun was high in the sky and hot.

Mr. Graves looked at the beeswax-capped frames Jamie had stacked inside the freezer. "They'll need to freeze for a couple of days before we can cut the honey into chunks," he said. "That'll prevent wax worm."

"What's wax worm?" Jamie asked.

"Nasty scavengers that burrow into the wax and wood of the frames," he explained.

Jamie was glad to be out of the bee yard and even happier to take off the hot overalls and gloves. When Mr. Graves took away her veil, she almost felt like herself again.

Mr. Graves seemed a different man when he worked in the bee yard. He was patient and kind instead of unreachable or sarcastic, as he'd been before.

Gus came running up to the honey house. "Come look at what I've done," he said.

They followed him to the fountain. He'd pulled all the dead lily pads out and stacked them on the grass. Only a couple of inches of dirty water sat in the bottom.

"You *are* a good worker, Gus," Mr. Graves said. "Let's have a glass of lemonade and cool off. We'll work on this tomorrow."

Jamie turned on the hose and washed her hands off.

Mr. Graves came out of the house with three glasses and a dazzling emerald decanter full of lemonade. They sat at the blue table in the shade of the fig tree.

Gus chattered to Mr. Graves about his goldfish. Jamie watched the scraps of black cloth blowing in the breeze in the bee yard while she drank her lemonade.

"Why do you have black cloth tied to the hives?" she finally asked.

Mr. Graves looked out to the bee yard. "When someone in the house dies, there's a saying that you have to tell the bees right away or else they'll take sick and die off, too. Or maybe they might just leave. I don't know if I hold with these superstitions. I don't know if I'm trying to be on the safe side or because maybe doing it makes it a fact that Pearlie really died."

"Are you a hermit?" Gus blurted out, his eyes wide.

"Gus!" Jamie cried.

"No, boy," Mr. Graves said. "Hermits live in the woods by themselves in shacks. They talk to toads and snakes, or a possum if one happens to come calling."

"Well," said Gus, "people say you're a hermit. Even Pearlie said so."

Mr. Graves actually smiled at this. "Pearlie was known to exaggerate from time to time."

"Um," said Gus, "why don't you go places more?"

"There's no place I like to be more than here. It wasn't always this way."

"What way was it?" Gus persisted.

"You're a nosy bones, Gus," Jamie muttered.

"Well," said Mr. Graves slowly, ignoring Jamie, "it was this way: We had a son, Pearlie and I, named Mason.

He was a fine boy, but he died a long time ago. I've been living my whole life since then in my own backyard, tending the bees and the flowers. It suits me."

Jamie was shocked. "Pearlie never told me you had a son."

"Sometimes there's real hurt in memory," Mr. Graves said. "It's like a toothache, as bad as that. We moved to this house after Mason died, and Pearlie got busy with people at her honey stand, and I just kept to myself and tended the bees."

They were quiet for a while, watching the lines of bees flying back and forth between the hives and the creek.

Finally Mr. Graves said, more to himself than to them, "I've outlived Mason and I've outlived Pearlie. Now all I have to do is outlive my grief."

Jamie's mother told her once that sadness, if expressed, lost some of the power it possessed when kept in secret. But Mr. Graves's confession left her unsure of where to put her gangling arms and legs, or what to say.

Suddenly Mr. Graves put a finger to his lips. In the oak tree were three blue jays, blue as blue could be.

"Blue jays," whispered Gus.

"Pearlie's favorite bird," said Jamie.

They sat watching them. One hopped to the edge of a branch and flew off. The other two followed.

"Three of them for three of us," Gus said.

"That's a sign from Pearlie, no doubt," Mr. Graves said, his face grown soft.

They made peace without words.

"We'll come and help you tomorrow and some afternoon next week," Jamie offered.

* * *

When they were back in their own yard, Gus stopped her before they went into the house.

"You know that place under the pecan tree where Mr. Graves buried that Skunk cat?"

"Yeah," Jamie said.

"While I wasn't paying attention," Gus said, "Tank dug it up. Know what was in there?"

"What?"

"Not a cat but a skunk, a *real* skunk," Gus whispered loudly. "I covered it back up and sent Tank home. I almost told you a million times."

"I'm glad you didn't." Jamie pulled up a stalk of grass and chewed it thoughtfully. "Skunks are pretty destructive. Maybe he killed one that was hanging around the bee yard and buried it."

"Why do you think he told us Tank killed his cat?"

Jamie looked back toward Mr. Graves's yard. "I don't know, but he seems lonely. He was a lot nicer today than he was the night I took the cake over."

"He hardly ever waved at us before Pearlie died," Gus said.

"Mother said he'd need people," Jamie said. "He really needs help in that bee yard, too."

94

Chapter
NINE

Jamie sat at the back of the classroom in a circle with Frederika, Theresa, and Abigail. Mr. Hughes-Walter handed Theresa a paper and moved on to another group.

Theresa sighed and wrinkled her nose. "The question is, 'If you caught your best friend cheating on a test, should you tell on her?'"

"Well," said Abigail, "that question doesn't apply at St. Agnes because no one ever tells on anyone anyway."

Theresa leaned forward and whispered, "These questions are always about snitching. You know the only reason he's making us discuss these stupid topics is that he can't get anyone to tell him who painted his padlock and about all the other things that are happening around here."

Mr. Hughes-Walter had invented a subject he called Moral Development. Every afternoon for an hour the class broke up into random groups of four and discussed things like: Was it okay to tell the authorities if your parents beat you with a rolled-up newspaper? If your sister shoplifted, would you be obligated to turn her in to the store management? Should you tell your best friend's parents if she was engaged in an illegal activity?

"If you ask me," Frederika said, "the honor system is turned inside out at St. Agnes."

"What do you mean?" Abigail asked.

"Think about it," Frederika began in her know-it-all tone. "At most schools if you see a classmate cheating, stealing, or doing anything wrong, you're honor bound by a code or something to tell on them."

"So what's your point?" Abigail asked.

"My point, Abigail," Frederika said as though she were talking to a first grader, "is that at St. Agnes you're honor bound by some unwritten code *not* to ever tell on anyone about anything."

"Oh, shut up, Frederika," Theresa said.

"Yeah," said Abigail, "you'd probably like to go to a school full of snitches."

"You shut up!" Frederika shot back. "Both of you just shut up and excuse me for living!"

"Someone *should* excuse you for living," Abigail said.

Moral Development wasn't working out very well, Jamie thought. This was only the third day, and someone in every group would regularly get overinvolved in the debate, become white-faced, and finally tearful. Already the high-pitched din in the room had Mr. Hughes-Walter racing from group to group making calming noises.

Jamie took *The Pigman* from her desk and put it under her arm. Mr. Hughes-Walter looked far too distracted to care if she left for a while. Feeling somewhat downbeat by all the bickering, she slipped out the door and headed for the bathroom. She was surprised when Kai rushed past her in the hall and went in first.

Jamie hesitated at the door but finally decided she had as much right to be there as anyone, even Kai. When she entered, Kai was at the bathroom sink, her breath coming in short, wheezy gasps. She fumbled in her shirt pocket and pulled out a plastic inhaler. She frantically puffed on it, shook it, and puffed again. A look of wild-eyed panic crossed her face. Something was very wrong.

"What can I do?" Jamie asked.

"This one is empty. Go to my locker," she said in a raspy whisper, "the one on the bottom by the classroom door. Get another inhaler."

"What's the combination?"

"It's three–thirty-seven–three. Hurry!"

Jamie ran to the locker and fumbled with the combination. The door finally flew open with a bang that echoed down the empty hallway. She rummaged through the messy contents until she found two plastic inhalers at the bottom.

In an instant Jamie was back in the bathroom. Kai's face was ashen, her breathing strangled. Jamie thrust one of the inhalers into her hand. Kai shook it, puffed from it, then dropped it to the floor. She grabbed the other from Jamie and gasped in the medicine. Her face was anxious as she held it in her lungs. Finally, she raggedly breathed out, waited, then gasped into the inhaler again.

Kai's face relaxed somewhat and her breath deepened. Still, Jamie was frightened. "Do you want me to get Mr. Hughes-Walter?"

Kai looked at her, eyes ablaze, and violently shook her head. When the door opened and a younger girl came in, Kai scowled at her, an expression of white-hot rage in her eyes, and hoarsely whispered, *"Leave!"*

The little girl backed out the door. Her running footsteps reverberated against the walls. Jamie felt weak-kneed with relief. If Kai could frighten someone out of the bathroom with a whisper and a scowl, maybe she was getting better.

Jamie pulled paper towels from the dispenser and ran cool water on them. When she tried to press them against Kai's forehead, Kai pushed her away.

"I need to go outside," Kai said shakily. "It's too stuffy in here."

Jamie followed her to a bench in the courtyard. "That poor little girl probably peed in her pants," Jamie said.

Kai smiled a little, still wheezing.

"My friend Mary Lieta from my old school has asthma," Jamie said. "She has an inhaler, too, and she told me it was really scary when she couldn't breathe."

"Look." Kai leveled her unsettling eyes on Jamie. "Thanks for helping me, but no one outside my family knows about this, and..."

"I knew about it," Jamie interrupted.

"What?" Kai looked incredulous.

"Sure," Jamie said. "You were wheezing at Zoe's house. I didn't think much about it, but you sounded just like Mary Lieta."

"Did you talk about this to Zoe?" Kai demanded.

"Why would I talk about asthma with Zoe?"

"I don't know," Kai said, shaking her head. Jamie

thought she was becoming increasingly nervous. "Just don't, and don't tell this Mary Lieta friend of yours either."

Jamie's mouth fell open. "Mary Lieta moved to Florida after school was out last year."

"Well, I don't want to talk about any of it. I *hate* this asthma, I *despise* it, and I don't ever want to talk about it." Kai leaned back against the bench and closed her eyes. The asthma attack had left her pale and weak.

"No problem," Jamie said, raising her hands.

Kai's eyes flew open. "It's gotten a lot worse in the last few months."

"Oh," was all Jamie said.

"No one could even tell I had it before; it was so mild."

"You don't need to be embarrassed about it," Jamie said.

"Do *you* have it?" Kai asked in a demanding tone.

"No," Jamie said.

"Then be quiet," Kai said.

"Okay," Jamie raised her hands again. "But if you ask me, you sure do have a lot of secrets."

"I didn't ask you, and that's totally ridiculous."

Watching Kai, back in control again, Jamie realized something she thought was important. Kai's power resided in her attitude. Even when she was sick or frightened or jealous, she behaved as though she was in charge.

Jamie felt braver still. "Well, I don't think most people would keep something like asthma a secret from their very best friends. Then there's that circle thing Abigail was talking about in the bathroom."

Kai looked at Jamie with a faint sneer, as though she

had a mashed bug on the side of her face. "You want me to tell you about the circle in exchange for your keeping your mouth shut about my asthma."

"I wouldn't blackmail you," Jamie said. "Sure, I want to know about the circle, whatever it is. But if you don't tell me, I'm not going to talk to anyone about your asthma."

"Sure," Kai said, rolling her eyes.

"I promise I won't," Jamie said.

Kai heaved a deep sigh. "Let me think about this." Jamie knew Kai didn't trust her. She didn't even trust her own best friends with information about her asthma.

"Okay," Kai finally said. "It probably would have happened eventually anyway, but it's not that easy. There's something you have to do first before you can find out anything. Everyone has to do it. If you're afraid of heights or blood, just say so now and we'll drop the whole thing."

"I'm really not afraid of anything," Jamie said.

"That's a bald-faced lie, Jamie," Kai said, the old cutting edge restored to her voice. "Everyone gets scared and you know it."

"Not me," Jamie bragged. Somehow she knew this strategy would hook Kai. "It's like I was born without the knowledge of fear. I would probably be a great warrior."

"I guess we'll just see about that, won't we?"

The bell rang and girls in green and white spilled out of the building doorways.

Mr. Hughes-Walter made a beeline for them, followed by Zoe and the twins. "Did you think you could skip out on Moral Development completely?" he said, an angry tone in his voice.

"I didn't feel well, and Kai found me in the bathroom," Jamie said.

"Did you go to the nurse?" he asked.

"Well," Jamie said. "I was embarrassed. It's a girl thing."

Mr. Hughes-Walter colored, and the veins in his forehead pulsed. "The next time you don't feel well, tell me before you leave class. Is that understood?"

"Yes, sir," Jamie said. She looked down.

He walked, stiff as a ruler, back into the building.

Kai made a fist of her hands and put both thumbs up. "Thanks," she whispered.

She quickly changed the subject. "Pukes-Walter is losing it. He's even started taking Billy the box turtle home with him every night."

"What's going on? Where were you?" Merit asked.

"Jamie is going to jump the big oak tree at Black Angel Bridge, and you know what that means. Right?" Kai said firmly.

"I think it's great!" Zoe said. "But she's never been there. She won't know how to do it, and it's really dangerous."

"What could be so dangerous?" Jamie asked with false bravado.

"Black Angel Bridge is on property that Kai's grandparents own," Merit said. "There's a huge oak tree there. We've been going for years, and Kai's big sisters taught us how to jump from a rope swing into the river."

"That doesn't tell me why it's dangerous," Jamie said.

"You have to swing out and let go of the rope at just the right time," Vivica said.

"So?" Jamie said.

"The river is only deep in the middle," Zoe warned. "If you let go too soon or too late, you could break both your legs by jumping into shallow water."

"Sounds like fun." Jamie smiled tightly. Pearlie Wu told her once that the white spots in your fingernails meant you were untruthful; one spot for each lie. Jamie kept her fists clenched; it was hard to protect yourself when your fingernails stood ready to betray you.

"Worse than that," Vivica said, iron-colored eyes somber, "if you chicken out and don't let go at all, you'll pick up speed on the way back and smash your skull to smithereens on the tree trunk."

Kai shrugged, looking at Jamie. "My sisters and some of their friends did it. We've done it."

"Why the gloomy forecast, then?" Jamie asked.

"You'll be the first person *we*'ve ever taught to do it," Merit said. "It *is* part of the deal, though. That and the blood."

"Part of the circle deal?" Jamie asked.

"That's enough information for now. Are you still up for it?" Kai asked.

Jamie knew she had to live up to the brave image she had bragged about to Kai.

"Of course I'm up for it," she said with a reckless smile. "I'm not afraid of any old bridge or tree." She clenched her fists so that her fingernails were hidden in her palms and felt her stomach turn over like an egg in a skillet.

"Okay, then," Kai said, "after school on Friday we'll ride to Black Angel Bridge. We can stash our bikes and stuff at Zoe's house before school. It's the closest to St. Agnes."

* * *

Jamie had a couple of days to puzzle her fate. If other girls had jumped this huge tree and lived to tell about it, were Zoe and the twins exaggerating the danger? Kai appeared to think it was easy, but would she care if Jamie got hurt? And what did *blood* have to do with it?

What she did know was that she had been hanging around on the edges of friendship since school was out last year. With Pearlie gone, she was as lonesome as the streets of the moon. She especially wanted to be Zoe's friend, and she knew it could never really happen unless she somehow won Kai's trust.

The rest of the week at school, no one mentioned what was to happen on Friday, but it was never out of Jamie's mind for long. She was grateful there was a distraction, even a minor one.

Someone had taken Heever, a small brown lizard, from his terrarium in the kindergarten room. He scampered in the large bowl of narcissus on Mr. Hughes-Walter's desk. A long thread tied loosely around his leg was knotted around one of the many tall spears of green with white flowers. Heever seemed happy zigzagging through the wet bed of multicolored pebbles.

Mr. Hughes-Walter clearly didn't know Heever was there. Merit was the first to expose him. She whispered to Jamie, "Heever's in the narcissus. Pass it around." Jamie passed it back to Theresa, and on and on it went from girl to girl until Vivica fell into uncontrollable laughter at the back of the room.

"What on earth, Vivica?" Mr. Hughes-Walter thundered. He had developed a twitch in his right eye. "Stand up and tell us what is so darn funny that you have to disturb the entire class again?"

"I was doing my worksheet," Vivica said, standing, obviously trying to control herself, "when someone, and I swear I don't know who, came by and whispered, 'Beavers want to kiss us.' It just struck me..." She suddenly sat down, put her head in her arms, and laughed loudly again.

Now the whole class was laughing. Mr. Hughes-Walter's face was flushed, and his eye twitched.

For the next two days the girls found reasons to go to Mr. Hughes-Walter's desk and ask unimportant questions so that they could see what Heever was up to. Lump finally discovered the little lizard and batted at him during a vocabulary test. This broke the class up again. Mr. Hughes-Walter took Heever back to the kindergarten.

It was just another prank, but this one was different for Jamie. She liked knowing a secret, even if she didn't exactly know what the secret was. At least she would get the chance to find out, but the closer Friday came the more often the words "jump" and "blood" haunted her thoughts.

Thursday afternoon, when she and Gus finished helping Mr. Graves, Jamie asked, "Have you ever heard of Black Angel Bridge?"

Mr. Graves frowned. "I took a swarm of bees from there several years ago. It's not too far from here, but it's a place so wild the hoot owls holler in the daytime."

Jamie felt weak as a kitten. "My mother is going to

take Gus to the eye doctor tomorrow. I know she'll be busy when they get back, and I have something I have to do. I don't think I'll be home until dark. Could Gus come over here after his appointment?"

"Why not?" Mr. Graves shrugged.

Just before bedtime the phone rang. It was Zoe. "Would you come with your bike a little early in the morning?"

"Sure," Jamie said.

"I want to tell you some things," Zoe said quietly. "Make sure you know what you're doing."

Jamie hung up and got in bed. She lay still, a wax doll, staring at the ceiling. Her brain tumbled as it had each night since hearing about Black Angel Bridge. Just the name sounded impossibly menacing. She wished she'd never heard of it. Even more, she wished the jump were over and she knew if all this dread and worry had been worth it.

Chapter 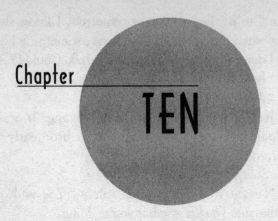 TEN

Early the next morning before school Jamie rode her bike to Zoe's house. She wore her swimsuit under her uniform and took a bag with a towel.

Zoe came out with her books and said, "Let's leave before the others drop their bikes off. I want to talk to you alone."

They started down University Avenue toward St. Agnes. A wind from the east whipped Zoe's hair around her face. She kept brushing it back impatiently.

"My hair freaks out every morning when I wake up," Zoe said.

"Mine looks like I stuck my finger in an electric socket," said Jamie.

A serious expression suddenly crossed Zoe's face, and she looked up at Jamie. "Tell me the truth. Are you afraid of heights?"

"I don't even know," Jamie said. "On the one hand, all of you have jumped into the river and lived to tell about it. On the other hand, you and the twins make it sound so dangerous—what with broken legs, smashed skulls, I don't know what-all. It sounds like there's a good chance I could end up like Humpty Dumpty. I've been pretty nervous about it, but don't tell the others."

"That's why I wanted to talk to you," Zoe said. "What I wanted to tell you is this: Jumping the big oak tree doesn't have to be so dangerous if you do it right. I'm going to jump first. Watch me. When it's your turn, hold on *tight* to that rope, and don't look down. Just swing out, and *don't look down*. Then let go when you hear me yell 'Let go!' Got it?"

"I'll try," Jamie said.

"That's not good enough, Jamie. You won't get away with being a slow learner in this situation. You have to do it. I'll go over it again when we get there."

They walked in silence for a few minutes. Because they were early, they sat on a bench in front of the university.

"Kai likes you, Jamie," Zoe said, "or you wouldn't be doing this jump today."

You don't know about the asthma attack is what Jamie thought. "I guess it's important that Kai likes me?" is what she asked, and immediately regretted it.

An awkward look crossed Zoe's face. "If everything goes the way I hope it will, it is important. The thing is this, Jamie. I really like you, too."

"Is Kai as bossy as she seems?"

"My mother calls her the Clique Commander, even though she likes her," Zoe said thoughtfully. "Kai is complicated and she fights change. But she's always been the one full of plans and ideas. When we were little, she made up the most amazing games, and she's still at it. She's bossy, but she's loyal. Things would be pretty boring without her."

They got to school as the first bell rang. Zoe squeezed Jamie's arm before they went inside the classroom. "Nothing will ever be the same after today," she said.

Jamie gave her a wan smile in return.

The rest of the day was hot and long. The lump in the pit of her stomach seemed to grow larger with every passing hour. Jamie got through it by drawing up a long and detailed Last Will and Testament. In the end, she left everything to Gus. Just before school was out, she folded the will and placed it in her desk.

When they met back at Zoe's house after school, all five bikes were in the garage with their bags. They'd all worn their swimsuits under their uniforms. The bags were full of towels and snacks.

"Let's get started," Kai said impatiently, taking off down the driveway.

Kai pedaled down University Avenue, scattering red and yellow leaves in a whirlwind of confetti, followed by Vivica and Merit. The twins rode side by side, laughing. They had the ability to do the same sound effects—fry like bacon, whine like mosquitoes, jingle like a charm bracelet.

"What's this?" Vivica asked Merit, making a long, creaking sound.

"A tree growing," Merit answered.

They glanced behind them at the baffled expressions on Jamie's and Zoe's faces and giggled all the way past Booger Hollow until they were pedaling on the side of the Braxton Highway.

Kai turned abruptly onto a narrow farm-to-market road. A truck roared past, leaving a trail of little dust cyclones. They came to an incline, and Jamie had to throw all her weight on the pedals to go uphill. Clover fields, as green as if someone had recently painted them with a brush, were on either side of the little road. The day was so hot it hummed, and Jamie's uniform stuck to her back.

Kai finally stopped under a big pecan tree by the side of the road.

"This is it," she said to Jamie. "See that sign that says 'Private Property'? We've got to climb the fence and pull the bikes under. Then we take Little Spur Trail." She pointed to a narrow unpaved road.

Jamie's handlebars got stuck beneath the wooden fence, so the twins helped her maneuver her bicycle under. They were quiet now as they rode down the dirt trail that wound like a ribbon through the brush. The smell of dust and goldenrod was in the air, and insects hummed around them. Jamie thought of Gus having his eyes checked at the doctor's office and then planting new lily pads with Mr. Graves. She wished she were with him.

The road dropped suddenly down to the riverbank, where the water was brown and swift. The air was filled with the sound of rushing water and the breeze sighing high up in the oak trees. The road went gradually uphill for a time and was crossed with the cleft, heart-shaped tracks of a deer. Abruptly an ancient covered bridge came into sight. The bikes bumped as they entered the bridge, which was dark inside, with crisscrossed beams supporting the roof. Going slowly through the gloom, Jamie heard the hollow, wooden echo of their passage.

When they came out of the dark tunnel of the bridge, they rode to a soaring oak tree by the edge of a cliff overlooking the river. Rough wooden pegs led up the black trunk to a thick branch. A rope hung from a larger limb above it.

Kai straddled her bike and pointed. "You have to climb out on the lower limb and grab the rope above it. Spring out as far as you can so that you fall into the middle of the river."

Jamie looked over the side of the cliff. The river narrowed and flowed swiftly below. When she looked back up at the branches of the tree, she was flooded with fear. The afternoon, in a stroke, seemed impossible and endless.

They sat on an outcropping of rocks and pulled their uniforms and sneakers off. Jamie's head felt peculiarly light, and sounds from the river came to her as muffled. She couldn't say anything.

"The main thing," Vivica urged, her eyes suddenly narrowed in concern, "is that you have to let go when we say. Timing is everything."

"Remember, if you freak out and don't let go," Kai said, "you'll swing back and slam into the tree trunk at top speed and probably die."

This sent another jagged slice of fear through Jamie.

"Kai!" the other girls said in unison.

Kai took a big drink of her Gatorade. "Well, I'm just reminding her for her own good. Do you want her to end up like a smashed pumpkin or something?"

"I'm not going to freak out." Jamie gave Kai a bold look. Inside she feared she was on the verge of bolting.

"Don't worry about the rope breaking or anything like that," Merit said. "Just concentrate on dropping when you hear us yell."

"I'm going to do it once for you to see," Zoe said.

Zoe jumped over a rock and scaled the pegs on the tree trunk. She scrambled out to the lower limb and grabbed the rope. Hesitating for a fraction of a minute, she pushed off and swung out above the water.

"Now!" Zoe yelled to herself, and the girls watched her let go and fall into the water.

Zoe bobbed instantly to the surface. She swam hard against the current to the shore and clambered up the steep bank. Her shiny copper hair was a mop of wet curls framing grave eyes.

"Good show," Kai said.

They surrounded Jamie again. Zoe folded her arms, her teeth chattering, and said, "See? When we tell you to drop, just drop."

"Whatever you do," Kai said in her bossy tone, "don't look down. Understand?"

"Sure," Jamie said.

Her heart hammered so loudly she could barely hear the water. She slowly climbed the pegs and crawled out to grab the rope. The branch was narrower than it looked from the ground. Without thinking, she looked down at the water so far away, and for a moment the idea of jumping into the rushing water was more frightening than the thought of swinging back only to hit the tree trunk.

"Don't look down!" she heard Kai yell.

Jamie remembered that her mother sometimes accused her of not understanding consequences. Well, she understood that everything from the tree branch break-ing to the river carrying her downstream to swinging out so far that she couldn't hear them tell her to drop was a consequence.

Dizzy, blood pumping hard, she grabbed the thick rope and whispered to herself, "You told Kai you weren't afraid of anything, so prove it."

Jamie shut her eyes tight, swallowed hard, and flew out and up into the sky. She felt a fierce thrill until she heard "Let go!" She froze. The rope was on its way back to the tree when she heard the girls yell "Let go!" again at the top of their lungs, terror in their voices.

She dropped the rope and fell through space. Tips of branches scraped her legs and then she smashed into the shallow part of the river and felt the thick mud below her feet send a jolting shudder through her leg bones. The water near the bank was pale green, and a dragonfly landed for a moment on her arm, then rose in the air, its electric-blue tail flashing.

Jamie got control of her feet and stood stock-still on the bank, green ooze coming up between her toes. She felt shorter and smaller, and her shins throbbed. She looked down to see her scratched shins bleeding into the water. It doesn't matter, because I did it, she thought. I didn't do it perfectly, but I did it.

Jamie climbed up the bank, the muscles in her legs jumping.

"You scared us!" Merit said.

"Your legs are bleeding!" Zoe said, handing her a towel.

"I'm fine," Jamie said. "They're just scratched from the

tree branches." She rubbed the blood from her legs with the towel, too shaky and cold to show relief.

"We told you to drop—*twice*," Kai said.

"I don't think I heard you the first time," Jamie lied.

"Hey, not bad," Kai said. "But I'm still the only one who dropped exactly in the middle of the river the first time."

"She's right," said Vivica, laughing into the teeth of the wind.

It seemed to Jamie that a collective sense of relief seized the group.

Vivica and Merit raced to the tree, and Kai followed. Zoe sat with Jamie and pressed the towel against her shins until she stopped bleeding.

"Were you scared?" Zoe asked.

"What do you think?" Jamie looked at Zoe.

"I know I was. I was the last one to jump, and Kai's big sister had to go out on the limb with me."

For the next half hour the air was filled with squeals and splashes. After a time, Jamie got her nerve up again and climbed the tree to the rope. She swung out, and at the top of the swing she felt as if she was flying, weightless in time. She dropped into the shimmering water when she heard the girls yell, "NOW!"

The others clapped for her as she swam toward the shore. As she stepped onto the bank, she sensed something behind her. She looked back as a snake S-curled through the water.

Their side of the river was in shadow now. Goose bumps appeared up and down Jamie's arms. The girls wrapped themselves in towels and sat together on the rocks as the color of the sky changed from blue to pink and purple.

"You did great, Jamie," Zoe said softly, and smiled. "I'm proud of you."

"Thanks," Jamie said. "I felt like Tarzan."

Vivica did a good imitation of a Tarzan yell.

Merit said, "No, it's like this," and yodeled louder, sending the birds squawking from the trees.

"I'll draw the circle now," Kai said. She grabbed a small bag and dropped from the rocks to the ground.

Chapter ELEVEN

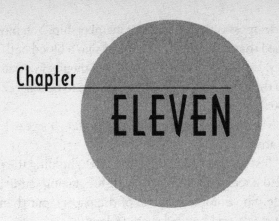

The carefree mood seemed to change immediately. Vivica and Merit shifted apprehensively on the rocks while Zoe twirled a strand of hair. What now? Jamie wondered.

Kai looked around on the ground and found a stick. She drew a large circle in the soft dirt under the tree. Merit jumped to the ground and went over to Kai. Heads up, they searched the mammoth tree trunk.

"There it is," said Kai, and pointed.

Merit leaned over, laced her fingers together, and boosted Kai up to a large knothole in the tree trunk. Kai thrust her hand inside, brought out a bundle of folded papers, and dropped them to the ground. Then she hopped off Merit's hands.

Vivica and Zoe nodded to Jamie. They took her to the circle, and Kai placed her inside it.

"Sit," Kai said.

Jamie sat across from Kai while the others arranged themselves around the outside of the circle. Jamie felt self-conscious and shy, hugging her bare arms.

Kai said, speaking to Jamie, "We are the Secret Circle.

Fearlessness is the first test for membership. You have just passed that one. Now you have to sign a blood oath of secrecy. Even if you decide not to be a member or you don't pass the other test, this oath binds you to be forever silent about the Secret Circle."

"I want to be a member," Jamie said. "I swear I won't tell anyone."

"Just saying it isn't enough." Merit, holding the pile of folded papers, traded places with Kai, facing Jamie in the circle. She unfolded several of the papers, put them in a neat stack, and handed them to Jamie.

Most of the pages were old and faded. One by one Jamie read the words printed in ink. "I, Liz Standish, promise never to tell about the Secret Circle." "I, Karen Frank, promise never to tell about the Secret Circle." "I, Dezi Jacobs, promise never to tell about the Secret Circle." Each page was signed in blood.

Fascinated, Jamie read page after page of the same vow written by girls she didn't even know until she came to the newer pages with the same pledge written by Zoe, Kai, Merit, and Vivica.

"We did this last summer when we decided to start the circle again," Merit said.

"Who are all the other people?" Jamie asked, handing the papers back to Merit.

"Kai's sisters started the Secret Circle when they were at St. Agnes," Merit said. "It's really important that no one finds out, because the school doesn't like it. Secret clubs are against the rules."

"Here," Kai said, handing an open pocketknife to Zoe.

"No," Zoe said. "I can't do it."

"Can't do what?" Jamie's heart quickened.

Kai shrugged and changed places with Merit again. "Are you right- or left-handed?" she asked in a matter-of-fact way.

"Right," Jamie said.

Kai took Jamie's right index finger and turned her hand over.

"Wait," Jamie said, pulling her hand back. "What are you going to do?"

"Cut your finger so you can sign the secrecy pledge, stupid," Kai said, taking Jamie's hand back.

Jamie averted her eyes and bit her tongue. She felt a sharp slice and looked down to see her blood drip on the ground.

Kai unfolded a sheet of paper that read just like the others: "I, Jamie McClure, promise never to tell about the Secret Circle."

"Sign the pledge," Kai ordered.

Jamie was pretty sure Kai had cut her finger deeper than she needed to. She pressed it into her already-bloody towel, took the paper, and signed her name in blood, though it was smeary and not that easy to read.

"Good," Kai said, and waved the paper in the wind to dry. Then she folded it up and put it with the others. She and Merit put the papers back in the knothole.

They stayed there above the river for a time. With Zoe and Kai and the twins scattered beside her, a wave of warmth swept through Jamie. It had to do with a sense of belonging. She could feel they were happy for her, maybe even Kai. Jamie believed for the first time since coming to St. Agnes: There is more that is right with me than there is wrong with me.

As they got ready to leave, Jamie asked, "What do I have to do next?"

"The loyalty test," Zoe said. "Sometimes it's the hardest one, but you'll do fine. That's when we'll tell you more about the purpose of the circle."

On the way back to town their shadows were long and black on the dusty road. When they stopped at Ashton Road, Zoe said, "We'll see you Monday at school."

"Congratulations!" Zoe called as Jamie turned on Ashton Road.

"You did it!" Vivica yelled.

Ashton Road was dark except for the streetlamp in front of her house near the end of the road. Here and there a few people sat on their front porches. Pale yellow light from inside the houses shone on them.

Jamie had thought this day would be as impossible to get through as playing the piano with her teeth. It seemed as though she'd left for school days ago instead of just this morning. A gnawing worry suddenly interrupted her excitement and relief. What would she have to do for the loyalty test and when would she have to do it?

The weekend winged by. Jamie helped her mother bake a huge groom's cake for a wedding that Sunday night. The thick chocolate icing was sprinkled with candied violets and iced pansies that were fashioned by hand.

On Monday morning Mr. Hughes-Walter put up a poster board. CAREER WEEK was at the top in neatly printed block letters. He had done away with "Moral

Development" without explanation. Maybe he thought "Career Week" would work out better.

"If either of your parents, a relative, or a friend has an interesting career they would like to share with the class, please choose a time during history and geography and invite him or her to come. It would be fascinating if they brought artifacts or pictures of their vocation."

Jamie thought of her mother hauling the huge mixer down the halls of St. Agnes. Her face colored at the thought. Of course her mother would bring batches of cookies and probably a cake. The class would like that. Jamie dismissed the idea. Mrs. McClure didn't have time for Career Week with all the weddings and parties she had to cater.

The twins offered their father, a pediatrician, but not their mother, the child psychiatrist. Theresa's father was the mayor. She wanted him to come and talk about the mayor's duties.

Jamie looked at Zoe, who smiled at her and shook her head. "Maybe my father could bring a dead person," she mouthed, and fell over limp in her chair to demonstrate.

Jamie was shocked at first, but she was beginning to understand that Zoe wasn't flippant about dead people so much as about death and her family's business.

"My mother is the head of the English department at the university," Holly Wright declared.

"So what?" Sandra March snapped. "It doesn't make her a better English teacher than my father. He writes papers about Shakespeare all the time." So many students had parents who taught at the university, including Kai's father, that there was some bickering over how many people were needed from the teaching profession.

Mr. Hughes-Walter clenched his jaw as the arguments waged on.

"It's going to be boring to have all these teachers come," Frederika Potts said. "I, for one, would never be a teacher."

This drew angry looks from several classmates, as well as from Mr. Hughes-Walter.

"What I mean is," Frederika continued, "we need people from a lot of different professions, or we won't really learn anything."

Mr. Hughes-Walter looked like a tall, wilted celery stick with glasses. He sighed. "Why don't we talk with the parents and friends, see who is available, and if there is such a stampede to sign up, we'll worry about it when the time comes. Really, girls, we cannot get so upset about everything."

All the bickering put the class in a collective bad mood. Kai came down Jamie's row to sharpen her pencil and whispered, "Be at Zoe's house tomorrow afternoon. We have something to talk about."

Jamie couldn't keep the smile from her lips. It was hard to believe she was no longer so alone at school. When she looked up from her work, Abigail Frank, her lips pressed tight, stared at her. She caught Abigail looking at her at lunch, puzzled, as if trying to decipher a mystery.

Exotic smells came through the back-door screen when Jamie walked in from school. She heard the hiss of the iron before she saw her mother humming at the ironing board.

"What smells so great?" Jamie asked.

"Probably it's the curry in the Indian food I made for a dinner party tonight," Mrs. McClure said. "The tandoori chicken is the best I've ever made!"

"Where is Gus?"

"Next door with Mr. Graves." Mrs. McClure motioned with her chin. "He got his glasses this morning, and a boy in his class already knocked them off him."

"I'll just go over and check," Jamie said, and gave her mother a quick kiss on the cheek.

She pushed through the hedge and found Gus and Mr. Graves in the garage. Gus's new glasses were lopsided on his nose when he ran to her.

"We filled this burlap bag with sawdust," Gus said, his voice awestruck. "It's going to be a punching bag so that I can practice my jabs."

Mr. Graves tied a tight knot around the top of the bag, threw the rope over a rafter, and pulled the bag up even with Gus's chest. He fastened it in place and stood back.

Gus went into a crouch, jabbed at it lightly, and thumped his right fist into the bag. He bounced around on his toes, jabbing, hooking, snuffing through his nose.

"I can't see Gus as a fighter," Jamie muttered to Mr. Graves. They walked to the honey house.

"Neither can I," Mr. Graves said. "He can work out his frustrations punching at it, though."

"Did you do that for Mason?" She immediately regretted this question, but it was too late. Jamie wished she wasn't so nosy.

"Yes, I did," Mr. Graves said as gently as feathers falling. "Mason was small like Pearlie. He hated school, wasn't good at it. The punching bag helped some."

The confidential tone Mr. Graves used when he answered Jamie's questions made it like the giving of a gift, the gift of self-revelation.

The honey house was warm and fragrant.

"I took the frames out of the freezer to drain this morning," Mr. Graves said.

The honey frames lay on wire squares. They were scattered on the worktable and the floor. Several fat glass jars with lids sat empty in boxes. Jamie got a pair of rubber gloves from a corner cabinet. A framed quote she'd never noticed jumped off the wall above the cabinet and punched her in the eye. It said: "We forfeit three-fourths of ourselves to be like other people."

"Forfeit means give up, right?" Jamie asked.

"Yes," Mr. Graves answered.

She read the words out loud to Mr. Graves.

Mr. Graves ran hot water into a tub. "Schopenhauer said that. He was a philosopher who lived a long time ago."

"Do you think that's true?" Jamie asked.

"Yes, I do," Mr. Graves said. "It's easier and maybe not as lonely in the short run to fashion ourselves like other people and go with the crowd. In the long run, though, it's a very sad thing not to be authentic, our true selves."

"Is that why you're a beekeeper?"

"It suits me," Mr. Graves said. "I feel peaceful when I work outside with bees and flowers. Pearlie felt more alive working with people, and that was authentic for her."

"What if people don't accept you when you're not like they are?" Jamie asked.

"Eventually they usually will," Mr. Graves said. "It just takes time."

Mr. Graves dipped a jagged knife in the hot water, wiped it with a cloth, and cut the first comb into squares. Jamie pulled on the rubber gloves and carefully tucked the sticky squares into the clean jars and filled them with honey.

Pearlie strolled through her memory. She could still see Pearlie struggling under the weight of the big plastic containers when she carried them to the honey stand so that Jamie could open the spigot and fill the jars with honey.

After a time they traded jobs and Jamie cut the combs into squares.

"Who's going to sell this honey at the stand?" Jamie asked.

"I am. There's no one else to do it. I have to come out of my shell now that Pearlie's gone. I haven't any choice," Mr. Graves explained with a kind of desperate dignity.

Somehow she knew he wanted to ask Gus and her to help, but he was too proud.

A vision of Mr. Graves speaking to the class for Career Week rose up, and Jamie smiled. Her thoughts shot in several directions. Who had a more unusual job than Mr. Graves? And if he wanted to come out of his shell, it would be good for him. Mr. Hughes-Walter would be thrilled. Weren't bees insects, and weren't insects science? She thought so.

"You know," Jamie said, "my teacher is having Career

Week. We can invite speakers to come to school and talk about their work."

"Oh?" Mr. Graves obviously didn't think this had anything to do with him.

"Yeah," she said, nodding, more and more pleased with the idea. "I was thinking that you have the most interesting career of anyone. You could bring some of your things and talk to us about beekeeping."

Mr. Graves abruptly set a jar down on the worktable. "I'm not much for public speaking." He cleared his throat with such a harsh harrumph that Jamie started.

"You wouldn't have to talk for long," she said to quench the sudden panic in his blue eyes. "The class asks lots of questions, and all you'd have to do is answer them."

He shook his head. "I don't think so, Jamie."

"Please," she begged. "It would be good for all of us. Gus and I will help you at the honey stand, too."

"I'll think about it," was all he said.

A long silence followed, which Gus broke when he burst through the door. "There's a special-delivery man at the gate! He's got a package for you, Mr. Graves. It has 'Live Insects' written on it."

Mr. Graves's blue eyes lit up, and his face crinkled into a smile. He quickly wiped his hands on a towel and hurried out of the honey house to the gate.

"What kind of live insects are in here?" the delivery man asked, holding the box away from himself.

"Bees," Mr. Graves said. "Italian bees."

The delivery man quickly passed the package to Mr. Graves, who signed for it.

Jamie and Gus followed Mr. Graves back to the honey house, where he put the package on the worktable.

"Open it," Gus urged as if it were a birthday present.

The brown paper wrapping had holes punched in it. Mr. Graves carefully tore it away. Inside was a screened wooden crate. One side held a grapefruit-size cluster of bees; the other, a small cage with one large bee.

"More bees?" Gus asked.

"These are a rare breed of Italian bees, boy," Mr. Graves said softly. "They're gentle as kittens and superior honey producers. I'm going to build a new hive for them."

Mr. Graves took out the separate little cage that held the queen. She was a beautiful red-gold color and had a glossy green mark on her thorax.

"Isn't she hungry?" Jamie asked.

Mr. Graves indicated a feeder can inside the small cage. "It's full of sugar water."

The cluster of bees buzzed against the screen. To quiet them he painted sugar syrup on the screen and let them take all they wanted.

"This queen set my pocketbook back," Mr. Graves said. "But she's already mated and ready to start laying eggs. She could change my entire operation."

"When are you going to put the new bees in their hive?" Gus asked.

"Let's see." Mr. Graves looked at the ceiling. "I'd say Friday is about the right time. Meanwhile, I'll observe them. Make sure they're healthy."

Jamie watched Mr. Graves. She'd never seen him excited before or even really happy. His eyes actually twinkled.

"You know," she said. "I bet my class would love to see that queen. Mr. Hughes-Walter says it's interesting if you bring things to look at for Career Week."

"You think so?" Mr. Graves asked.

"I know so," she said. "You could come during history and geography tomorrow. Mr. Hughes-Walter would be so glad not to have to talk about Zebulon Pike. He calls him a bumbling fool."

"Who's he?" Gus asked.

"He's the bumbling fool," Mr. Graves said, "who set out to find the source of the Mississippi River and ended up a year later at a peak they named for him, Pikes Peak."

Jamie smiled. "See, you and Mr. Hughes-Walter already have something in common. History and geography starts at eleven."

Mr. Graves set a fan up in front of the boxes to keep the new bees cool. He moved it around several times.

Jamie knew he wanted to show off the new queen.

"Please?" she said again.

"I'll be there," he said.

Chapter

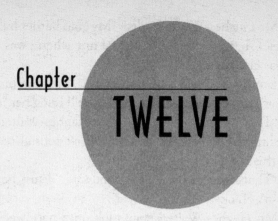

TWELVE

Jamie caught Mr. Hughes-Walter in the hall before school the next morning.

"I hope you don't mind," she said, staring at the squiggles on his tie, "but I invited my neighbor to come for Career Week. He's coming today."

Mr. Hughes-Walter pulled down his glasses and looked at Jamie over the top of them. He tucked his wrists under his armpits. "Jamie, there's a sign-up poster in the room. Career Week starts on Monday. *Next week*."

"I know, but if he had until Monday to think about it," Jamie said, "he'd probably back out. He has this really unusual profession."

"Who is this person?"

"It's Mr. Graves, and he's a beekeeper," Jamie said in a hopeful voice. "Remember? His wife, Pearlie Wu, died. I think it would be good for him to tell us about what he does."

"You say he's a beekeeper?"

"Yes, sir," Jamie said. "He has about thirty hives, and he sells honey and comb honey, too."

Mr. Hughes-Walter smiled. "My grandfather had bee-hives. Oh, just a few, but I helped him when I was a boy. It was fascinating."

Jamie felt relieved. "It *is* interesting. And he got a new Italian queen bee yesterday. I think he'll bring her."

"This is fantastic, Jamie," Mr. Hughes-Walter said. "Ordinarily, I'd be upset that you didn't consult me first, but this is a wonderful opportunity."

"That's what I thought," Jamie said. "I just hope he doesn't chicken out."

Mr. Hughes-Walter's face took on a narrowed look. "Now, you did tell him eleven A.M.?"

"Yes, sir," Jamie said.

"Well, I'm sure he'll be here," her teacher said, and walked away down the hall whistling an unrecognizable tune.

Now that she had Mr. Hughes-Walter's approval, Jamie couldn't shake the new worry that Mr. Graves might change his mind and not show up. Or what if he did show up and had absolutely nothing to say? He'd clearly told her that he wasn't a public speaker.

Mr. Graves wasn't shy, exactly. It was as if he were a drop of oil paint and everyone else drops of water in a jar. He was just separate, and different.

The truth was that even though Jamie hadn't liked him very much at first, she now wanted him to be a part of her life because he'd made her and Gus a part of his backyard world. She'd gone into it thinking she had to, but somehow they'd all become friends in the process. He'd been especially good for Gus, too, and that had made Jamie's life easier.

She was preoccupied all morning with thoughts of Mr. Graves's visit and the Secret Circle meeting. When she saw Mr. Graves's frowning face at the square of glass in the classroom door, she jumped up without permission and went to greet him.

"I brought some things." Mr. Graves held a large cardboard box.

Mr. Hughes-Walter rushed over and introduced himself. "Come in, come in," he urged. "This is such a pleasure. I was something of a beekeeper myself as a boy."

Mr. Graves put the box on a table at the front of the room. "I've brought some samples for you to taste while I tell you a little about beekeeping."

He unpacked several small glass jars. In each one a slosh of golden honey surrounded a chunk of honeycomb. He'd even taped a plastic knife to each jar. In the box were loaves of store-bought bread, too.

These weren't the jars Jamie had helped him with yesterday. He was up all night getting ready for this, she thought.

Jamie turned to Zoe. "Would you help me pass all this stuff around?" she asked.

"Sure," Zoe said.

Once Jamie and Zoe had distributed the jars and bread, Mr. Graves wrote WINTER, SPRING, SUMMER, FALL on the blackboard. While the class ate bread and honey, he talked about the seasons and what bees and beekeepers do. He seemed nervous at first, frowning and clearing his throat several times. After the first few minutes, though, his voice became clear and strong.

Jamie was impressed. Giving the class something to

eat while he talked was genius. He's done this before, she thought.

"The most important part of the hive is the queen," Mr. Graves finally said. "She lays all the eggs and determines the entire future of the hive."

From the large box he lifted the screened cage that held the new queen. "This is an Italian queen bee. She's very valuable," he said.

"Why did you have to get a bee all the way from Italy?" Vivica asked.

A smile bent Mr. Graves's lips. "She actually came from a breeder in New Mexico. Every beekeeper wants to improve his honey. Italian bees produce superior honey, and they're easier to work with. This queen is from a rare breed of Italian bees."

"Did you have to take her away from the other bees to bring her here?" Frederika asked in an accusing tone, as though Mr. Graves had done something wrong.

"Not really. She came in the mail just yesterday—along with several workers in a separate box. I'm building a new hive now, and by Friday they'll be ready to go to work."

The bell rang for lunch. The class filed by to look at Mr. Graves's new bee and thank him as they left the room.

"You're going to be a hard act to follow, Mr. Graves," Mr. Hughes-Walter said.

"I'm glad I didn't invite anyone," Zoe said, holding the cage at eye level so that she could see the queen. "Everyone complains if your speaker is boring. No one could complain about you."

Mr. Graves blushed while Mr. Hughes-Walter laughed.

Jamie smiled. Mr. Graves seemed relaxed and content as he put his things back into the box. He'd been a huge success.

"Could you stay for lunch?" Mr. Hughes-Walter asked. "I'd love to hear more about all this. It brings back so many memories."

"I should get my queen back to the honey house," Mr. Graves said. "But come for a visit after school sometime, and I'll show you around." He looked at Zoe. "You come, too. Jamie and Gus are going to help me at the honey stand. They'll want some company."

Zoe's eyes lit up. "I'd love to do that. My mother and I buy honey from your stand every spring and fall."

Jamie walked Mr. Graves to his car. "I think you've done this before," Jamie said.

"A long time ago, when I was just getting started," Mr. Graves said. "I gave talks to clubs. It was a way to advertise so that people would buy my honey. I always took samples. Pretty soon people just knew where we lived, Pearlie and I."

"Thanks so much, Mr. Graves," Jamie said.

A troubled look crossed Mr. Graves's face. "There's something I ought to tell you. Maybe this isn't the right time."

"What?" Jamie asked.

"You remember the day I called you and Gus over about the dead cat?"

"Sure. How could I forget?"

Mr. Graves rubbed his beard and hesitated. "A skunk had been raiding my hives. I had no choice but to shoot

131

it, and I buried it. When I saw Gus in the tree that afternoon, something about his face and his movements reminded me of Mason, of everything I've lost, really. I was lonely, and I don't have Pearlie's way with people. I think I forgot how to make friends a long time ago. I called you over on impulse. It was childish, but I'm afraid I lied to you and Gus."

Jamie considered telling him that she knew about the skunk, but instead she said, "That's okay. We might not have become friends."

"I'm glad you understand," he said. "Well, I'd better be on my way."

By the time school was out the sky was overcast. Clouds blew overhead as Jamie, Kai, and the twins walked with Zoe to her house.

Vivica tried to imitate Mrs. Willow, the music teacher, who sang in an operatic voice, but Kai and Merit seemed focused and full of purpose. Zoe hung back and walked quietly with Jamie. Every few minutes Zoe would break into Jamie's worried silence and say, "The hard part is pretty much over" or "You've almost got it made." This continual reassurance made Jamie even more nervous. It seemed as though Zoe was trying to convince herself as much as Jamie.

Zoe's room smelled like sunshine, even though an autumn wind puffed the curtains and the sky grew more overcast.

A golden pound cake was on Zoe's desk, along with a pitcher of milk and five glasses. Something about the fifth glass heartened Jamie. She was included, she had a place here, at least for today.

The twins dropped to the floor with Jamie. They kicked off their shoes and socks as Zoe poured the milk and handed everyone a piece of cake.

Kai flopped in an armchair, a leg draped over one side, bobbing around. Her shoes were off, too, and her toes were still painted different colors.

"We told you about the Secret Circle on Friday afternoon," Kai said, "but we didn't tell you why it was started in the first place."

Jamie nodded.

"The purpose," Kai continued, "is to be friends for life, to always know that no matter where you are or what you're doing you have a group of loyal and courageous friends you can count on."

Jamie felt a thrill.

"It's not that easy, as you know now," Kai continued. "I mean, you overheard that Abigail Frank's sister was a squealer even after she made the jump and signed the secrecy vow. She couldn't pass the loyalty test and got kicked out. We need to know that *you're* loyal."

"See," Merit said, "we've spent part of the summer and the first days of school proving ourselves. We got initiated on Saturday night."

Jamie scratched a spot on her skirt. "Does any of this have to do with pranking Mr. Hughes-Walter?"

"Yes," Kai said. "We're the ones that let the white mice out and planted the earthworms in Frederika's desk. We don't know what happened with Heever, but we gave Lump the Mohawk. Everyone knows I painted

Mr. Hughes-Walter's padlock black. Those are just a few of the things we did."

"Will anyone else get in?"

"Sure," Zoe said. "Some other girls will get in eventually. You're the first one besides us who gets to try."

"What else do I have to do?" Jamie asked.

"You've shown you're fearless by jumping at Black Angel Bridge," Vivica said. "Now you have to prove that outside of your family, your loyalty is to the Secret Circle."

"How do I do that?" Jamie asked.

"We'll decide that today," Kai said. "I say we do the same thing for Jamie that we did for ourselves. We'll each write a suggestion on a piece of paper."

Merit looked at Jamie and added, "We put them in a bowl or something, and you draw one out. The one you draw is the one you have to do."

"It won't be anything unreasonable, will it?" Jamie asked, feeling suddenly uneasy.

"I guess it depends on what you think is unreasonable," Zoe said, and handed her another piece of cake. "But the dangerous thing is over."

Merit rummaged through Zoe's desk and found notebook paper and colored pens. She handed a piece of paper and a pen to each of them, including Jamie.

"Why do I get one?" Jamie asked.

"You can write one for yourself," Merit said. "But if you happen to draw it and we decide it's too easy, you have to draw again."

Zoe pulled an empty goldfish bowl out of the cabinet under her bookshelves. "We can put the suggestions in here."

Jamie took a bite of cake and thought. She had the sensation of dry warm crumbs passing across her tongue, but she couldn't taste anything. What if she exchanged Mr. Hughes-Walter's box turtle, Billy, for Gus's little one? Maybe Mr. Hughes-Walter would think Billy had shrunk. He'd really be steamed. That would show her loyalty, wouldn't it? It might be funny, too.

She wrote: "Exchange Billy with my little brother's small turtle." Jamie wondered if this was bad enough. Zoe sat with her pen clenched in its writing angle, her brow creased. She hadn't written anything yet, but Jamie knew whatever she suggested would be easy to do. The twins wrote, their eyes lit with brightness. Vivica's idea would probably be funny—embarrassing maybe, but funny. Merit's would be funny, but probably harder. Kai folded her paper and put it in the goldfish bowl. She smiled, not exactly at Jamie. It was an unfocused smile, impersonal.

Don't let me get Kai's, Jamie prayed.

Jamie folded her paper and put it in the goldfish bowl. By the time the others had tucked theirs into the bowl, Jamie's stomach hurt.

"All righty," Kai announced into the silence. "Time to pick, Jamie."

Vivica stuck her hand into the bowl and mixed the folded papers up. "Now cover your eyes."

Jamie put one hand over her eyes and the other one into the bowl. Her pulse raced as she drew a folded paper out.

She slowly unfolded it and read, "Get the bee."

Chapter

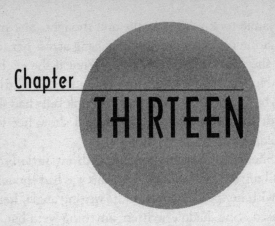

THIRTEEN

Later Jamie would remember how dumb she had been.

"Get the bee," Jamie read out loud. "Get what bee?"

Vivica and Merit exchanged glances and Merit mouthed, "Wow." They both looked at Kai.

Zoe reached over and touched Jamie's wrist lightly. A troubled look creased her forehead. "Mr. Graves's bee. The one he brought to school today."

The little line in Zoe's forehead was a furrow now. She actually turned and glared at Kai for a brief moment.

"I can't do that," Jamie said. "That's like stealing something really expensive and valuable."

"You were *sooo* unlucky," Merit said. "You got Kai's."

Vivica added, "Kai's suggestions are always the worst. I got hers, too. I had to stay in a casket downstairs for an hour. I thought I was going to have a mental heart attack."

"But you have to admit," Merit said, "she gave herself a bad one when it was her turn. She drew her own. None of us would have made her paint Mr. Hughes-Walter's padlock black. He was so mad, he would have sent her to Miss Pickney if he'd caught her."

Zoe nodded, her green eyes troubled. "Miss Pickney would have at least suspended her. I was certain she'd get caught."

"That padlock wasn't expensive," Jamie protested. "He got it replaced, and it didn't mean anything to him."

"Well, he had to have the custodian take it off with a bolt cutter," Merit said. "He had to buy another one, so in a way it was expensive. He's been a nervous wreck, afraid someone is going to mess around with the new one."

"Yes, but Mr. Hughes-Walter's wife didn't die just a few weeks ago," Jamie argued. "He's not a friend, either."

"True," Zoe said. "That's very true."

"Yeah," said Vivica in a rush. "I forgot about that."

In spite of the open window, the room seemed close and stuffy. Jamie stared at Kai, hoping for a sign that she was kidding.

"Look." Kai finally spoke in a calm voice. "Don't steal the bee. All you have to do is borrow it. He said he wasn't going to put it in the hive until Friday. If you get it tonight, I'll meet you here at Zoe's really early in the morning. We'll look at it to make sure you did it, and you can have it back before he even knows it's gone."

Jamie pulled her skirt over her knees and rocked. Kai made it sound easy, but Jamie knew it wasn't. She gave the group a pleading look. "What if I draw two other suggestions and promise to do both of them?"

"It doesn't work that way," Kai said.

Panic booted Jamie in the stomach. This is all my fault, she thought. Why did I talk Mr. Graves into bringing the bee to school in the first place?

"Well, what if I say no?" Jamie asked. She felt as though her face were on fire.

Kai's back stiffened. She dragged a finger across her throat. "You don't get in, that's what, Jamie. You wanted something reasonable? This is reasonable. For all we know, you'll go to him and ask him to loan you the bee for an hour. If he's such a good friend, he'll do it, too."

Jamie couldn't imagine asking Mr. Graves for his Italian queen. It would be like asking her mother if she could borrow one of her huge wedding cakes for an hour.

All of a sudden Jamie had an image of Zoe, the twins, and Kai walking down the halls of St. Agnes forever, without her. She thought of going back to her old private-citizen plan and bit down on the tip of her tongue. No way.

"Okay," she said, and turned to Kai with her mouth set. "I'll do it." Even as she said it doubts assailed her like tiny devils.

There was a sudden glad outbreak of talking. Their voices climbed over one another's as Jamie looked at the floor and rubbed at the polish on her toenails. She couldn't think of a thing to say. They wanted her to be in the Secret Circle. Even Kai looked relieved.

Jamie gathered her shoes and backpack and rose slowly. "I have to go," she said. "I'll see you here in the front yard at six tomorrow morning, Kai."

"Good luck," Merit called.

Jamie glanced behind her. Zoe followed her down the stairs. They went outside into the gray daylight.

"I'm sorry you got Kai's suggestion," Zoe said.

"I am, too," said Jamie. She looked over Zoe's shoulder.

"You can do it, Jamie," Zoe said. "Where does he keep the bee?"

"In the honey house."

"What if it's locked?" Zoe's eyes were like those green paperweights that had amber lines of glass streaked in the middle.

"It's never locked," Jamie answered.

"So no problem. Right? I mean, it should be easy," Zoe quickly said. "You just set your alarm and go over before it's light out. You take the bee, bring it here, and take it back before he gets up. Piece of cake," she added, a warm smile breaking.

Jamie was in no mood to stand around in the yard and listen to Zoe's pep talk. She lifted her hand in an awkward wave and walked down the street. It was glazed with mist, and her feet were cold.

After all, maybe it *was* just borrowing. Mr. Graves did his exercises on the porch at around seven thirty every morning. If she met Zoe and Kai at six, she'd have more than enough time to take the bee back before Mr. Graves was up. She'd be home for breakfast. The bee would be fine, Mr. Graves would never have to know, and she'd be initiated. Still, a nagging sense of guilt left her feeling jumpy and irritable.

Jamie turned on Ashton Road. The fields were drenched with mist. A storm was coming in from the north, moving slowly. In the distance the sky looked like a giant shower curtain drawn by the hands of God. Jamie could see through it, enough to see the outline of the hills on the other side. White ribbons of lightning jumped between the clouds and hilltops. A cool wind rose up to shake the trees.

After dinner Mrs. McClure said, "Jamie, you look tired. Why don't you do your homework early and go to bed?"

"I'll do it in a little while," Jamie said.

"There's no time like the present, I always say."

"I know you do," Jamie snapped.

"What?"

"I know what you always say. I hear it often enough, don't I?" Jamie felt a pang of regret as she caught the hurt look on her mother's face.

The storm actually started much later, at bedtime, when sheets of rain swept across the roof. Jamie set her clock radio for five A.M., placed it on the table by her bed, and sat in the dark at her window seat. Rain ran noisily down the window glass, making a wavy world. She placed her hand against the pane, letting the storm pass just beyond.

The sky cracked brightly with lightning, illuminating the fish pond and wet lawn chairs in Mr. Graves's yard. Puddles of amber light spilled from the windows of his house.

I could still call and ask to borrow the Italian queen, Jamie thought. Almost immediately she dismissed the idea. Somehow she knew he wouldn't understand. A clap of thunder broke, and Gus ran up the stairs.

"*Jamieee*," he cried in the doorway.

She took his hands, and they sat on the bed. "Thor is coming, we don't care. Thor is coming, we don't care," they chanted again and again. Gus squeezed his eyes shut, and his hands clutched hers. When the thunder finally passed, they got under the covers.

The familiar sound of pots and pans drifted up from the kitchen as rain drummed on the roof.

"Mother is banging pots to wake the dead." Jamie was so nervous and jittery she felt she would explode.

Gus's eyes opened wide. "Can you do that?"

"What?"

"Wake the dead?" he asked.

"No, Gus. It's just an expression."

"Oh."

"Sometimes I wish I'd been born to a family in say, Norway, where it snows," Jamie said.

"I know it," Gus said. "But then I wouldn't be able to work at Mr. Graves's honey stand next week."

"You like Mr. Graves, don't you?" Jamie asked.

"Yes," Gus said. His voice was sleepy. He pulled his teddy bear close and shut his eyes. In the light from the numbers on the clock radio, she made out the hanging button of Teddy's right eye. It seemed to leer at her. His fur was worn and rubbed completely off in spots, as if he had mange.

"This world and one more," she said softly, and sighed. It was one of her mother's favorite things to say when life seemed confusing and unfair. What would her mother say about this latest escapade? Jamie remembered herself as a small child when she honestly believed that if she closed her eyes, her mother wouldn't be able to see her doing something naughty.

A new idea struck her.

"Gus," she whispered.

"Yeah?"

"You know how Mr. Graves's new queen bee is a different color from the others? It has that green mark on it, too."

"So?" Gus asked.

"If someone took a regular bee and colored it with Magic Marker," Jamie said, "do you think it could pass for the queen?"

"Those queen bees are a lot bigger than the others, that's all I know," Gus said. "Besides, bees don't like to be colored. They'd sting."

True, Jamie thought. She wouldn't fool anyone.

Her mind was such a jumble that sleep came in scraps, and loud colors and sounds punctuated her dreams. She was awake and terrified when soft music from the clock radio came on. Zero hour had arrived.

It still rained lightly outside. The here-and-gone moon shone between the dripping branches of the trees. Jamie had a new worry wedged in with all the others. What if the Italian queen got wet? Would the bee die?

She pulled on blue jeans and a dark blue turtleneck sweater. Shoes would get wet and make noise, so she decided to go barefoot. She carried her Windbreaker over her arm so it wouldn't rustle.

Jamie turned off the music and glanced at Gus. He lay curled toward the windows, still sound asleep. If luck was with her, he wouldn't wake before she got back. Tank would be closed up in the garage because of the rain.

She drew in her breath, avoiding the loose board on the stairs. Her bare feet made no sound on the polished floors. Jamie went straight to the back door and let herself out. She put on the Windbreaker and pulled the hood over her head.

There had been a time when Jamie was afraid of the dark like Gus. But that was in her childhood. Still, she drew a flashlight from her pocket. The only sound was rain dripping from the trees and a chorus of frog song.

The privet hedge scratched and stung her face as she pushed through. Jamie held herself rigid, willed herself invisible. She strained and took a long look around the dark yard. When she was satisfied that it was empty, she finally inched her way to the honey house and eased the door open.

She went carefully inside and moved the dead yellow eye of the flashlight around the room. And there, in the corner, was the box itself, in front of the electric fan, sitting cool and small and quiet, like the easy answer to a difficult question. Jamie's breath left her in a rush as she slipped the box under her Windbreaker and let herself out.

Ashton Road was dark but for the glare of the lone streetlight softened by a milky drizzle. She ran quickly down the hill to the intersection and up University Avenue. Rain from the hood of the Windbreaker dripped into her eyes, and she blinked it away.

Watery reflections of herself slid along storefront windows. Jamie caught sight of her stooped image scuttling down the street like a thief. Borrowing. Hah! She'd have to ask permission to borrow. She'd stolen the bee. She'd go anywhere and do anything Kai told her to do. She'd even steal from Mr. Graves, and he'd helped her with Gus. Zoe had said there would be more new members. What would the next one have to do? Jamie felt sorry for her already.

Even though it was chilly and raining, Jamie's face felt like a furnace when she reached Zoe's house. The sky was just beginning to lighten. Her watch showed fifteen minutes until six A.M. She huddled on the porch at Zoe's front door and pulled the box out.

The bee was beautiful in an ugly sort of way. It seemed fine. Jamie's feet and hands were stiff and cold. An eternity passed until she heard a fumbling at the latch on the other side of the heavy front door. It opened slowly.

Zoe flipped on the light in the hallway. She wore a white nightgown, and gold freckles dusted her shoulders. "You did it!" she said softly.

Jamie nodded, but remained silent. It wasn't anything to be proud of. Just then a figure moved lightly around the street corner and up the walk. Jamie checked her watch. At least Kai was on time.

"Let's see," Kai said.

Jamie held the box up and turned the flashlight on. Kai inspected the box and gave Jamie an approving look. "You can be initiated this weekend."

"Then what?" Jamie asked.

"Then you're a member," Kai said. She actually looked happy for Jamie.

"And after that?"

"You're one of us," Zoe said.

Jamie nodded, but there was a pressure in her chest that grew and grew like an inflating balloon. She turned and walked quickly to the sidewalk. When she glanced back, Zoe and Kai were in shadow, silhouettes on the porch. She ran all the way home.

Chapter

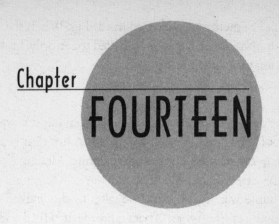

FOURTEEN

There was the smell of wet leaves and a soft patter of rain as Jamie pushed back through the hedge to Mr. Graves's yard in the raw dawn. Mud sucked at her bare feet as she flushed a bird that was roosting in the hedge. A small cry escaped her mouth when it flew up in her face like a bad dream and then was gone.

Just as she reached for the door of the honey house a wet nose nuzzled her hand. She looked down to find Tank sniffing for a treat. When he didn't find it, he pounced at her feet, yipping playfully. Jamie groaned. Tank had escaped the garage.

"Go home!" she whispered harshly, but Tank just skulked to the privet hedge and watched her with his head on his paws.

Breath suspended, Jamie opened the door of the honey house and closed it behind her. She turned on the flashlight and replaced the box in front of the fan. She quickly swung the eye of the flashlight to the framed quote on the wall. Was she giving herself up to belong to the Secret

Circle? Something quickened inside her. When she eased the door back open, she was relieved to see only Tank, still waiting for her by the hedge.

The sun came out of gray clouds on Jamie's walk to school. She tried to quiet the voice in her that repeated this question: Will I ever like Jamie McClure again? "Shh," she told herself. "Shh…"

Jamie was lost in dark thoughts as she walked down the halls of St. Agnes. Vivica and Merit talked with Kai and Zoe across the hall from the classroom door.

"Congratulations!" Merit called.

Vivica grabbed her wrist and pulled her into the group. "I would have been so scared."

Jamie braced herself and drew in a slow, deep breath. "I don't want to be initiated," she said, stunned by the suddenness of her own decision. She had not known that she would say these words until they were already spoken.

Zoe's brows pulled together in confusion. "What? Why, Jamie? You've got it made now."

"I just can't do it," Jamie said.

A tense, itchy silence hung in the air.

"You aren't serious," Kai said with a little laugh. The look of disbelief on her face said no one had ever turned her down.

"Yes," Jamie said, "I *am* serious."

"You should have thought about this before now, Jamie," Kai said.

"And *you* should think about the things you ask people to do," Jamie answered.

"You won't have to do anything else." The expression on Kai's face was dark now as she crossed her arms. "It will be someone else's turn next time."

"That's just it," Jamie said. "There *will* be a next time. You said other people would be chosen. No one should have to betray a friend to make other people happy. That's not loyalty. I don't want to make anyone else do something like that."

Kai's eyes held cold centers of anger, while Zoe raised her thumb to her mouth and bit the skin around the nail. There was a queasy silence.

"I'm sorry," Jamie finally said before walking away.

She took her seat in the classroom. She did her work as though she were a robot sealed inside a bottle and everyone else was outside. She didn't want to come out. At lunch she tried to read in the bathroom, glad for the solitude.

Jamie remembered the night she'd stayed over at Zoe's. A vision rose up of Zoe's face when Kai came over with the twins. Zoe might want new friends, but Kai would make it hard for her to have them unless she could call the shots. Jamie shook her head. She'd been so afraid of her old private-citizen plan, she'd almost given Kai the same power.

The class saw a menstruation movie during science. That's what it was titled: *The Menstruation Movie*. The school nurse sat in Mr. Hughes-Walter's chair at his desk. The movie was a cartoon of a talking egg. Jamie felt empty as she stared at the egg bouncing around the screen.

I don't want to be bossed around by Kai, but now I have no friends and Pearlie Wu is dead, she thought. Before Zoe and Kai and the twins, there was Gus and her

mother, and that was it. The cheerful egg talked endlessly, but Jamie wasn't listening. She felt like a pane of
glass that was cracked but still intact.

After the movie, just before the bell rang, Mr.
Hughes-Walter said, "Will you listen to me? I'm talking
to you, Jamie."

"What?" Jamie asked.

"When I talk to you, I want you to listen," he said.
"You've had potatoes in your ears today. I hope you come
back tomorrow with a different attitude."

The rest of what Mr. Hughes-Walter had to say
sounded like nothing to Jamie but blah, blah, blah. He
dropped his fountain pen into his pocket, bare nib down.
She watched ink blossom on his white shirt while the class
hollered, "Mr. Hughes-Walter, your shirt!"

That evening it rained again. Jamie avoided her
mother and paid only the slightest attention to Gus until
bedtime.

After Gus plugged his elephant night-light into the
wall, he faced Jamie with wide eyes. "Eddie Potts said his
big brother brought home the fifth-grade *Weekly Reader*.
Know what it had?"

"What?"

"All these pictures and writing about a scientist in
Germany who's been mixing stuff together from human
beings and hamsters."

Oh, boy, thought Jamie, even less in the mood to hear
Gus's fears than usual.

"Anyway, he's invented a humster. It's huge and hairy
with a stubby tail, and now the scientist knows it was a mistake because the humsters have a lot of babies every few

weeks. These humsters are taking over Germany, and some have escaped to America, and they have sharp teeth."

Jamie rolled her eyes. "And you believed this?"

Gus got a sly look on his face. "No. Eddie Potts is a fart."

"Well," Jamie said, "at least one good thing happened today."

Friday was worse. Mr. Hughes-Walter's latest tactic was strict academics. His lessons had become increasingly harder, as though he thought this would keep the mysterious incidents in check. He began a science unit on compounds, drawing diagrams on the board. Waving his thin hands in the air, he spoke endlessly about atoms and chemical elements. While he distributed a handout, a paper ball hit Jamie's arm and fell to the floor by her desk. She picked it up and opened it.

Can we talk? Please?

Jamie looked over at Zoe and shrugged. Zoe had a hopeful expression on her face. She knew Zoe wanted her to change her mind.

Mr. Hughes-Walter's handout contained charts that had to be read from the side, the top, and the middle. Complicated comprehension questions followed.

Instead of working on the comprehension questions, Jamie wrote "Humster" on the top of the page and drew a detailed picture of what she thought a humster would look like. She colored the humster with map pencils.

Mr. Hughes-Walter scowled as he collected the papers. When he saw Jamie's, his scowl deepened and he said sarcastically, "I can see you're much too advanced to work on my humble comprehension questions. Maybe you think you should be teaching this class yourself? Your attitude may be contagious. Why don't you spend the rest of the day in the library?"

I don't care, Jamie told herself, collecting her books. I really just don't care.

She sat at a library table and tried to read. A younger girl sat across from her. With a shy grin the little girl handed Jamie a dictionary with a scrawled note that said, "If you want to read something that will shock you, turn to page 85."

On page 85 was written: "Electricity. Ha-ha!"

Jamie gave her a forced smile and passed the dictionary back. She went to the librarian, Mr. Fenster, who was shelving a trolleyful of books.

"I have a library book," Jamie said, "but I can't concentrate. I was a library helper at my old school. Do you want me to shelve some of those books for you?"

"Are you kidding?" he said. "I'm so swamped I'd pay you if it wasn't against the rules."

She took the trolley to the stacks, looked at the spines of the books, and began putting them in their places. Abruptly an assortment of memories beset her. She thought of Zoe's laughing face on the steps to the embalming room, Vivica and Merit's urgent instructions before she jumped into the river from the big oak tree, and Kai's perfect face, pale and worried after her asthma attack.

The girls had kept her mind off Pearlie's death and filled the empty place inside with daydreams, adventures, and secrets.

Overwhelmed with loss, Jamie sat on a stool in the empty book-lined aisles. Hot tears streamed down her face. She wished she could talk to Pearlie. She wished there were an easy way to belong and still be herself.

Zoe caught up with Jamie after school and walked along University Avenue with her. The leaves were turning, and the university campus was a smoky autumn gray and gold.

"I know what we asked you to do was wrong, Jamie. I'm sorry, but..." Zoe turned her palms up and sighed.

There was a silence, and Zoe continued, "You used to like the idea of the circle."

"I know. It was a case of mistaken identity. I thought I was someone I wasn't."

"I don't know how to explain this, but things were different and special with you around," Zoe said. "Can't you just think it over again?"

"It wouldn't do any good," Jamie said miserably, "but thanks. It was mostly fun for me, too. I'm just not cut out for it." She paused before leaving Zoe on the sidewalk.

"We were friends before I knew about the circle," Jamie said. "I wish we could be friends like that again."

"Well," Zoe said carefully, "maybe we could some day."

Jamie took the weathered and faded HONEY FOR SALE sign off the hooks of the honey stand. She didn't feel like facing Mr. Graves yet, even though he didn't know

151

she'd betrayed him. She decided not to tell him for now. He'd had enough disappointments.

In the garage were sheets of sandpaper and green, red, and white paint left over from a birdhouse she'd tried to build last spring, without success. Jamie spent hours on Saturday and Sunday painting the sign white and lettering the words in green and red. Later she found Mary Lieta's address in Florida and wrote her a letter. Sunday afternoon she mailed the letter at the corner.

When she started back down Ashton Road, she was shocked to hear Kai's voice call her name. Kai wore cut-off blue jeans, a T-shirt, and cowboy boots. Even in this outfit Kai appeared as intimidating as ever.

Jamie waited for her in the road.

"What are you going to do now, Jamie?" Kai asked, hands on her hips. "Are you going to tell everyone?"

"I signed a pledge in blood," Jamie said. "I wouldn't betray that."

"You'd better not, Jamie, because—"

Jamie interrupted her. "Don't try to order me around, because it won't work anymore."

Kai's face was a mixture of confusion and amazement. There was a pause while she gathered her thoughts and took a deep breath. "I was going to say that when you signed the pledge and passed the tests, it sort of made you a member no matter what. You can't tell anyone anything at all."

"I'm not going to tell about your asthma either. That's what you're worried about, isn't it?"

"Maybe," Kai said. "It just isn't anyone else's business." She looked around the neighborhood. "I've always thought this street was kind of pretty, but unusual. It's right in the middle of everything but set apart. It's different like you're different."

"Well, I don't try to be."

"This really is about that old man and the bee? You felt *that* bad about taking it?"

"Yeah," Jamie said, nodding. "I felt awful about that and even worse about ever saying I would do it. I guess I don't take orders very well. I never even knew that."

Kai shrugged and shook her head. "Maybe you'll change your mind—and then again, maybe you won't." She gave Jamie a vague smile and walked back up University Avenue. When she came to the first cross street, she turned and waved. Jamie watched her as she became smaller and smaller.

Jamie got the sign from the garage and took it to Mr. Graves's house. It looked good, she thought, but she was nervous. He hadn't asked her to paint it. What if he didn't like it? When he opened the door, she held it up for him to see.

He came out from behind the screen door and pulled on his beard, looking at it. "*You* did this? For me?"

"I sure did," Jamie said. "Do you like it?"

"Why, Jamie! I'm at a loss. I think it's just grand."

They went to the honey stand, and she hung it back on the hooks for him to see.

"It was pretty faded, you know," she said.

Mr. Graves stood back and admired the sign. "I think it will get a *lot* of attention. That's what we want since we're down here at the end of the road. I've taken out an ad for comb honey in the *San Lucas Express News*."

Jamie was surprised. Pearlie never put ads in the paper. "If you advertised, we'll be hopping. Lots of people will want comb honey for holiday presents. I'll run the honey stand for you next week after school if you want," she said. "You'll need a break."

Mr. Graves suddenly seemed puzzled. "You've been so busy. How are you going to find time for all this?"

"Well," she said, feeling an ache in her throat. "I guess what Pearlie said was right: I am lonely. So I thought maybe if I kept busier it would help. I'm going to help in the St. Agonies library, too, before school and at lunch," she said.

"You don't sound too excited about that."

Jamie kicked the dirt with the toe of her sneaker. "I didn't have being a library helper in mind, but I have to get involved. I have to start somewhere."

Mr. Graves didn't rush to say anything the way Pearlie would have. He just listened, and she felt relieved.

A hedge sparrow alighted on Mr. Graves's gate. Dark orange smudges merged and parted, separating into butterflies, like sparks in slow motion. A few landed on Mr. Graves's outstretched arm.

"Migrating south," Mr. Graves said.

Jamie took this as a good sign and smiled, looking at a dusky monarch butterfly on her hand. The world was suddenly more in focus than before. Life had come back around to Ashton Road, the honey stand, and her family. She would venture out again, but Jamie knew where she fit in for now.